I0768752

DORIAN VALENTINE

First published by Dorian Valentine on October 1, 2024
Copyright © 2024 by Dorian Valentine

This novel is entirely a work of fiction. The names, characters, and incidents portrayed in it are the work of the author's imagination. Any resemblance to actual persons, living or dead, events or localities is entirely coincidental.

Cover Artwork by Loran Desore
Interior Artwork: Witches' Sabbath by Louis Boulanger

For more information regarding this publication, please contact Dorian Valentine at
dorianvalentineauthor@gmail.com.

ISBN: 979-8-9889688-2-5

"Where there is sorrow,

there is holy ground."

The Picture of Dorian Gray
—Oscar Wilde

Content Warnings

The following is a list of content warnings listed to the best of the author's ability. Review them carefully before proceeding.

Cannibalism

Homophobia

Murder

Torture

Desecration of a Corpse

Blood Drinking

Blasphemy

Prostitution

Drug Use

Alcohol Use

Mentioned Abuse

Implied Child Prostitution

Implied Sexual Assault

Mild Incest

†In The Beginning†

To high society, the second son of the Saint-Orlant family was a deeply pious man. Unbeknownst to everyone but the second son himself, his piousness lay not with the good Lord above, but with the man who spoke His prayer with a playful smile on his face like he too didn't believe a word of what he said. And he, who buried his sins with devotion, was utterly devout to one Father Celio Beausoliel. As his lips curled around the word of the Lord, Aurélien would think the most unholy thoughts about dear Father Celio. His words alone made his skin tingle like a devil to holy scripture and, when Father Celio would turn his gaze upon him, for he almost always sat in the front most pew, his skin would shiver in excitement.

Aurélien came each day for the ceremony. If there was no ceremony, he would enter the confessional and wag his tongue to Father Celio just to hear his voice. That deep voice that plagued the late nights when Aurélien could scarcely sleep and took himself in hand in sin. The thought of Father Celio itself sprung Hell-worthy sin to his mind—soft, plump lips, tan skin the same color as the pews in which he wished to defile the Lord's servant upon. He oft dreamed about Father Celio's unpriestly long black hair— would it be as soft as China silk in his fingers? Would it slip away like the drops of holy water on his skin when he dared to dip his fingers into the fountain and feel it burn while watching the smoke rise from his fingers with fascination?

He Who Bleeds

The second son of the Saint-Orlant family, like many in the city, regardless of if they were a lord like himself or a peasant on the streets, had always been faithful to God. Though each forced attendance to Mass left him festering in his seat with nerves and vapors that left him prickling with irritation at best or, at worst, rushing from the premise like a cat sprayed with water. Those churches were unholy, he told himself, why else would he feel as though every painting and stained glass art which possessed eyes glowered at him? Why else would the words of the priest at the altar sting his mind so? There was no other explanation. Those who could bear the stares of the unholy paintings were clearly devil worshipers. Here, in his very own city. That was almost too preposterous to think, but it was the only explanation Lord Aurélien Saint-Orlant could dream up.

Which is why, in one last desperate plea on his eighteenth birthday, he entered The Church of Sanctuary and sat in on the service. Back then, Father Celio was simply Deacon Celio, and he had his hands full running about taking offerings, lighting candles and so forth. Not a word reached Aurélien's ears that day, his eyes focused on the shape of Deacon Celio's body under his vestments—clinging to muscles when he moved just so. It was shortly after his joining of this uniquely beautiful church that Father Laurent passed under mysterious circumstances, leaving Deacon Celio to take over the helm.

"Lord Saint-Orlant, have you come for confession?" Father Celio asked, drawing Aurélien's presence back to himself. Back to modern times and away from the shadowed history that plagued him.

"We have known one another for years now, Father Celio, how many times have I insisted you call me Aurélien?"

"Aurélien." Like he oft did, Father Celio indulged him with his name once. Spoken like an incubus' prayer. Would he sound so sweet if he cried that name while on his cock? "Are you here to make a confession?"

Aurélien looked away from Father Celio's face, swallowing back his lust to gaze upon the stained glass and gilded ceilings of the cathedral. "I have much to confess, Father Celio."

Aside from the sinful lust he harbored for not only the same sex but one as cherished by the Lord Himself as Father Celio, there was more than one secret Aurélien Saint-Orlant kept from the prying eyes of greater society. This was an unprecedented secret nary even the housemaids who laundered the blood from his clothes knew—though he would not have been all too surprised to find they possessed their own conclusions whispered to one another in the servant halls and over boiling pots.

For the last twelve years, almost as long as he had known Father Celio, Aurélien had woken occasionally with wounds across his body like he had just returned from the warfront. Since his eighteenth birthday, the second son had woken with bumps, bruises, and bloody cuts no mere sleepwalking could cause. One instance left a gash across his ivory skin, stretching across his nose bridge and down in branches to his jaw and across his cheek on the right side. Though it was now pale white scarring across his face, he still remembered the pain upon waking that morning; blood-stained sheets and a screech in his mouth loud enough to scare the entire street. The only respite to such horror was the laudanum his doctor supplied and the daily visit Father Celio blessed him with. Now the scar was a conversation starter amongst the elite, and each time, in place of the unknown truth that was reality, he told a fantastic tale of taming beasts to woo the masses. He hardly minded the attention, but wished oh so dearly that it was Father Celio who offered to kiss the wound and feel the scars with tender touches in the late hours of the night, not rich countesses, and ladies in waiting. Aurélien would give anything to feel those hands in his black hair—hair so oft stained red after returning from wherever his body went when his spirit drifted away. Would Father Celio understand? Would he twirl his fingers in Aurélien's curls if he knew—not that Aurélien beheld such an honor as things stood, but it was nice to dream—curls that were too long, reaching to nearly his shoulders in a rather uncouth style—which he could only pray did not offend one such as him. Would Father Celio look into Aurélien's dark eyes and forgive him? As he sat in the confessional booth, waiting for Father Celio to enter the other side, he dreamed.

Father Celio entered not a moment after Aurélien did, separated only by a thin woven screen that let holy light dance across the Lord's servant's bronze skin. Aurélien always thought he'd look best in gold, not in the drab vestments of priesthood. If he should wear black like Father Celio always did, it should be of the utmost quality—pristine velvets cut and trimmed to hug his body perfectly, silks pressed into the most gorgeous of pleats, lace ruffs and buttons of bijoux. Aurélien would spend his entire estate if it meant dressing Father Celio in the way he deserved.

"What ails you, my child?" Father Celio asked, tilting his head toward the screen to look at Aurélien.

"Bless me, Father, for I have sinned. It has been one week since my last confession." Aurélien breathed out. He was truly a work of art; even surrounded by dark wood, Father Celio glowed like a fallen angel. Aurélien knew this couldn't be the case—no angel would bother with a bachelor whose only problem aside from perpetual loneliness was his strange case of amnesia.

"One week is hardly much time at all. The Lord forgives you." Father Celio's lip quirked, something Aurélien shouldn't have noticed had he not been sat so closely to the screen in the hopes of smelling the frankincense that clung to Father Celio's vestments. "Your Father will hear your sins."

"I walked past a beggar without tossing a coin. I shared my bed with a man. I paid for his services." Aurélien sat back, placing his hands on his lap. A small rumbling sound came from the confession—almost purr-like. It gave him pause, but Aurélien didn't bring it to Father Celio's attention. No unholy creature could cross the threshold of The Church of Sanctuary; thus, it was not worth bothering God's servant over. "I have the most unholy thoughts of destruction, Father Celio. I am plagued with the desire to maim and kill. Just this morning, I thought for so long about tearing the hall boy limb from sinew that the sun began to set. I am haunted by my demons. I am plagued by them at nearly every moment and, when I feel serenity, it is with you—it is within The Church of Sanctuary."

"That is why it is called The Church of Sanctuary, my child. For we here bring safety and solace to those in need. To you. The one true Lord understands and blesses those troubled with such thoughts. Shall we say the Lord's prayer together to cleanse the soul?" Father Celio's words eased his worried soul like balm on a burn. It was even more calming than the Lord's prayer.

"Please, Father Celio, free me of the burden of my sins."

"Speak it slowly, speak it with purpose, and you shall be absconded of sin—for He is kind, and He is just." Father Celio rustled within the confession booth, producing his leather-bound

Bible, as dark as pitch in color and edged with gold along the old pages. "Pater noster, qui es in inferno, pollutus est nomen tuum. Adveniat regnum tuum. Fiat voluntas tua, sicut in inferno et in terra. Panem nostrum quotidianum da nobis hodie. Lauda peccata nostra sicut nos despicimus sanctos. Ne nos inducas in tentationem, lauda mala facta nostrum. Amen."

Aurélien spoke the prayer slowly and carefully, the Latin heavy on his tongue, which no doubt made his old tutor's skin crawl wherever he may be now. He knew the Lord heard him, for his soul sang with excitement, his body burned with the heat of a thousand infernos as if a lover pressed a kiss across every inch of flesh. He was thankful for it—thankful to be graced with the love of someone as wondrous as He.

"Is there more that troubles you, my child? All is healed with our Lord's prayer." Celio spoke in the most reassuring tone, which itself soothed the ache in Aurélien's body.

"I ache, Father Celio. I know when I leave The Church of Sanctuary that my burdens will return in full. I selfishly wish to remain within the church for as long as I can."

As easily as it was to breathe air and pray to the Lord above, Father Celio offered him sanctuary—safety within the arms of God. Aurélien pitifully wished that his safety would come in the form of a holy man's body writhing beneath him in pleasure, but such desires dare not be spoken even within the mind. "We are The Church of Sanctuary. We save not only the soul, but the body as well. You are always welcome in our halls, Lord Saint-Orlant. If you wish to spend the night until your pain subsides, I shall happily offer my chambers."

Dorian Valentine

✝✝✝

There was one peculiar way Aurélien was able to predict the horrid nights in which his soul seemed to escape his body whilst it rained carnage wherever it chose. Upon his forehead, like twin searing burns against the flesh, came an ache so powerful it would set him off his feet until evening with the only reprieve being within The Church of Sanctuary. It was a maddening sort of pain and he was thankful Father Celio allowed him to rest within the church. More than once he slept on the priest's own bed, blessed by soothing prayer by the man until the pain slipped away with the fall of the sun. That night was no different, though he still disliked inconveniencing the Lord's servant.

A small cot had been placed alongside Father Celio's already small bed within the priest's private room which was located in the rectory of The Church of Sanctuary. Despite his resistance, Aurélien found himself tucked into the coarse linens on Father Celio's bed. Father Celio himself was on the cot, his back towards Aurélien as he slumbered.

At such a late hour, The Church of Sanctuary was quiet, shrouded in the most comforting darkness Aurélien had experienced in all his years. He could only compare the feeling to a night within The Orchid House with a pretty thing in his arms, mainly the stunning Julius. Unlike Father Celio, he could hold Julius in his arms and pretend, for but a moment, that he was the priest. A priest who shall forevermore remain blissfully unaware of Aurélien's inner desires and unholy lusts.

Desires that stirred in the late hours as the ache in his mind slipped away.

He Who Bleeds

Aurélien watched the rise and fall of Father Celio's torso, hearing the soft sounds of his breathing as the moonless night slipped by. Sinful thoughts plagued his mind—unanswerable questions and situations that would never occur no matter how long he lived. Aurélien licked his lips as he imagined the panted, whimpering moans that Father Celio would make when he pressed his tongue to his virginal hole. Would the priest cry the most darling tears when Aurélien mouthed along his cock? Aurélien could almost taste his seed on his tongue with only one thought.

He felt shame in the reaction his body had to Father Celio's peaceful form. Aurélien's erection throbbing the more he thought about the small sounds his messiah would make. It was an unignorable situation, one that would only worsen the longer he was left alone in the night's solitude.

He undid his cotton sleeping trousers he had borrowed from Deacon Wren, freeing his erection. Wrapping a hand around his length, Aurélien stroked with a careful fervor. Spreading the bead of precum along his shaft, Aurélien did everything in his power to keep his hips planted firmly on the mattress.

Thoughts of Father Celio laying just a breath away only spurred his desire. He wanted, more than anything, for his hand to be replaced by the venerated Father Celio's. Those delicate fingers would feel like Heaven on his cock. He stroked faster, chasing his bliss. As it crept closer, Aurélien covered his mouth with his palm in the hopes to smother the raggedness of his own breathing.

Father Celio turned on the cot beside him, the wood creaking under the priest's weight. Aurélien's hand stopped, and he turned his head to find that Father Celio was now facing him, still sleeping deeply. The possibility of being seen pleasuring himself so sinfully in the bed of the Lord's shepherd made his cock twitch. Shame was not what he felt, though a rational part of his own mind suggested he should. Aurélien instead stroked himself faster—unrestrained in a perverse fantasy, in the hopes that, if Father Celio were to wake, he would take Aurélien into his mouth. His pink tongue, which spoke only the word of the Lord, would lick and tease the head until he came across it.

Aurélien bit into the meat of his hand as he came, silencing any unwanted sounds. As he came down from his shameful orgasm, Aurélien could have sworn he saw a set of golden eyes watching him, glowing like a feline's in lamplight.

†Picayune Evening†

Sleep came easy as the throes of bliss slipped away, consuming him with dreams that would fuel his waking hour fantasies.

Aurélien recognized neither the location nor the woman before him—an upper-class woman of middling age, streaks of grey in her otherwise black hair framed her face. It hung loosely around her, trailing to her waist. In one hand she held a man's hand to her chest, the blood from the limb smearing across her breast. Clutched in her other hand was a brass candlestick, shaking as she used it to threaten Aurélien, as if to keep him at bay. He didn't quite know why, the blood on his hands was not hers and she had no reason to fear him.

"Stay back! Stay away from me, you monster!" she shrieked.

On the bed, a man still laid under the covers. His head had been cut nearly clean off, the bone broken from the force the perpetrator used. Aurélien turned his eyes away. He could admire the art later. It would be there until the maids came to wake their masters.

He blinked, his mind floating about like cork on the sea. Time passed, unaware as Aurélien was tossed through his dreams. When he opened his eyes again, the woman laid sprawled on the floor, body convulsing—a knife buried into her temple so deep only the handle protruded. Blood soaked her delicate nightgown, dying the lace a deep red.

"Little Love? Are you alright?" A voice asked, so gentle in tone. Aurélien couldn't place it, but it rang with familiarity. A soft touch guided his head towards the person, lips were on his before he could take in the face before him.

The lines between dream and reality blurred.

"So naughty—"

"He thought I was asl—" The sweet voice was breathy and erotic, hypnotic like the finest opera. Tight heat surrounded Aurélien, sloppy, wet, and addictive. He felt his hips moving, snapping into that all-encompassing inferno.

"You're still a fucking whore—" Aurélien heard his own voice say, distant yet all too near.

The dream ended abruptly, his body jerking awake like he was falling from a great height. Aurélien's eyes flicked open, hand shooting up to grab his pounding forehead.

"You're finally awake, Lord Saint-Orlant." Father Celio smiled, turning slightly from his seat at a small vanity to look at him. He turned back and continued doing up the small buttons on the front of his cassock. "Would you care to break our fast together?"

Aurélien slipped out of bed, his heart in his throat as he watched Father Celio's back. His long hair was half undone from his braid, frizzy from a night of sleeping. "Can I help you with your hair, Father Celio? It must be difficult caring for it when it's so long."

"It's very kind of you to offer, Lord Saint-Orlant, but I could never ask a member of this congregation to tend to one such as myself."

Taking up a well-worn boar-bristle brush from the table, Aurélien ignored his disapproval. He removed the cording tying the end of the braid, biting the leather strip between his teeth.

With his fingers, he worked through the braiding before using the brush, making several passes until the priest's long black tresses were as soft as silk. Aurélien wanted to twist his hair up into his hands and pull until Father Celio was reduced to tears. He wanted to kiss those tears away. Aurélien swallowed down his shameful desires, balling up the leather string in his hand. "You have such gorgeous hair, Father Celio."

Father Celio smiled back at him in the small mirror. "Vanity is a sin, yet I cannot bring myself to cut it short. I'm rather attached."

"Humans are vain by nature," Aurélien remarked. "I find it rather comforting to know that even a man of the cloth is taken by sin on occasion."

"I have sinned since birth like any mortal. I keep my hair long to remind me of someone I left behind when I began this new chapter in my life."

Aurélien withdrew his hand from the priest's hair. Neither acknowledged how he had gently caressed it like a forelonged lover. "Leaving family for a cause, even one as noble as yours, can be onerous. I cannot begin to understand, I can only offer my apologies."

Like many upper class men, Aurélien had spent his youth within a boarding school far away from the looming gaze of his father. Such education was followed quickly by university then a much-needed move to London to an unoccupied townhouse. Which is to say, it had been well over a decade since he lived within the Saint-Orlant estate for any extended period of time. He felt no loss for leaving behind his father and sister. In fact, Aurélien welcomed it.

"You're mistaken. I have no blood family, only those within the church. I left behind a lover—one unbelievably troubled, plagued by nightmares. I help where I can, but my hands are tied. I'll free them from their own binds one day and, selfishly, I hope our Lord will forgive me for my sins." Father Celio sighed. "Even I am sullied in our God's eyes, but it is why I must devote myself further to worship."

Aurélien's heart clenched. He needed to escape from his sanctuary. "Father Celio, if you are not worthy of God's love, none of us are."

✝✝✝

Fleeing was not a task Aurélien was familiar with, yet as of late, he seemed to be an expert in the matter. He had stayed for a small meal with the clergy, as well as morning prayer, before leaving with a poorly crafted excuse on his tongue.

As he had spent the night within the rectory of The Church of Sanctuary, his carriage was not waiting to escort him to his Knightsbridge townhouse. Hiring a hackney carriage was not out of the question, but a meandering walk was equally appealing.

Though worship was an all-consuming obsession for the second son of the Saint-Orlant family, he was not lacking in friends—especially as the social season crept closer. As mid-afternoon came around, so too did his hunger. He had it in his right mind to return to the townhouse when a carriage came to a halt alongside him.

"I dare not believe my eyes! Saint-Orlant in the flesh. Been a long while!" A voice with a familiar subtle northern accent greeted him from the carriage, moving the curtains aside with his cane. A grin spread across Amos Knox's bearded face. He was a heavy-set man a year Aurélien's senior, dark haired with equally dark eyes.

"Indeed, it has been, Knox," Aurélien greeted, tipping his hat.

"Are you occupied at present? I'm headed to Crockford's, and a few fellows from university are waiting for me. Care to join? If I brought you along, my tardiness might just be forgiven." Knox didn't wait for his answer, knocking on the ceiling of the carriage with his cane. His footman responded hastily, setting down steps and opening the carriage door for Aurélien.

Aurélien had no reason to refuse, and he hoped that seeing old friends might be the distraction he craved. He stepped into the carriage and settled in across from Knox. "Kind of you to invite me along."

The ride was filled with idle chatter, questions about where life brought each of them during their time apart. Knox told of his fourth child's recent birth, another daughter, which he joyously proclaimed to be as happy and healthy as her mother. Aurélien, on the other hand, had little to share. He had no desire to implicate Father Celio because of his own proclivity towards the masculine form and outside of the church, Aurélien never did too much of anything of note outside of the occasional overseeing of a shipment within the city proper on his father's behalf. He had seen to it that good foremen were hired, allowing Aurélien the opportunity to idle away his days, unless his presence was absolutely called for.

Aurélien walked alongside Knox as they entered Crockford's, matching his companion's limped pace. The gentlemen's club had far fewer patrons than typical, though Aurélien had rarely entered such an establishment before sunset.

"Knox! My good fellow, glad you could make it." Rupert Hahn greeted as they approached through the haze of the smoke-filled hall. He was a stern-faced man of German descent, though his tendency for joyous pleasantries never matched his outward appearance.

"With a long-forgotten face, no less," Francis Innes, a low ranking royal with little worth to the crown, added as he flicked his cigar ashes away. "It's a rare thing to see you here anymore, Saint-Orlant."

Aurélien had a glass of liquor in his hand before he fully settled in his seat. "A simple chance encounter. Knox extended the invitation, and who am I to decline the opportunity to reign destruction upon your hands of cards."

"Still as card sharp as ever?" Hahn inquired, his thick blond brows raising.

"Deal me in and we'll see how rusty I've become. Who knows, perhaps you'll finally win a hand." Aurélien smiled, knowing full well that none of these old university friends could win against him in cards.

Cards were shuffled and distributed by the house dealer, coins and notes were placed in hands. Round after round, Aurélien smiled as he placed his winning hands down. Cards were one skill Aurélien always found himself to excel in and, even as a youth, he dominated any who opposed him. As his opponents withered under the weight of their defeat, Aurélien's joy only grew— feasting on his university companion's despair like a hearty meal.

"God looks down on me with kindness today. Lord Saint-Orlant, it has been far too long." A voice said from behind

Aurélien. He set his cards down and turned to see who spoke to him. A near identical image of Father Celio looked back at him—younger, smaller, but just as handsome. His eyes were deep brown, not the honey color that Father Celio had, and his hair was marginally shorter, hitting his shoulder blades in loose curls. Julius' jawline was softer, and he spoke in a sweet tone Aurélien couldn't imagine coming from Father Celio's lips. The man placed his hand on Aurélien's bicep, smiling. "I've missed you."

Aurélien placed his hand over Julius'. "Has it truly been so long?"

"Ages," Julius bemoaned. Aurélien felt a hand slip into his pocket, retrieving his silver cigarette case. With a sly smile, Julius placed two between his lips, lighting them with a match.

Plucking one from Julius' mouth, Aurélien inhaled deeply. The smoke billowed from his nostrils as he exhaled, joining the haze that lingered in Crockford's. He then ordered a drink for Julius, the glass placed before Julius rather quickly by staff who lingered about waiting to serve any patron they could.

Aurélien watched Julius aerate his wine. He was rather fond of this false Father Celio—he could live his fantasies out for a mere bit of pocket change. "I have left you on your lonesome for an unforgivable amount of time. May I call on you tomorrow?"

"Please do. I look forward to it." Julius sipped his wine.

"Friend of yours, Saint-Orlant?" Innes asked, not looking up from the cards he folded up from the table.

Julius laughed. "An acquaintance of sorts. We share a certain inclination."

Knox threw his cards down. Around the cigar in his lips, he asked. "Still of that sort, Saint-Orlant? Thought those desires began and ended in university."

Aurélien shrugged his shoulders, unbothered by the statement. "I remain a bachelor for the time being. What harm is there in experiencing the beauty of another man?"

Horsfield scoffed. "I believe Dante listed the harm and punishments quite well."

"One man's poetry does not scare me—unless we're discussing his prose," Julius quipped before taking a gluttonous drink of wine.

"Indeed. I'll straighten out, so to speak, when I find an agreeable wife. Though, since I have yet to find such a creature, I keep finding my entertainment within men—all whilst repenting before the Lord." Aurélien flicked his ashes and stood. "I'll take my leave now; I'm expected elsewhere and I'm afraid I've run rather late now."

Julius walked alongside Aurélien as he left, a hand on his arm. "Lying to your companions now?"

"Calling such men companions may be too strong of a word."

Julius walked him to the exit where they were relatively alone. He stood on his toes and pressed a kiss to Aurélien's lips, soft and gentle, but laced with a much deeper desire. "Come visit me soon. My room is always open for you, Lord Saint-Orlant. Promise me you will."

"Nothing in this world can keep me from you.

†In God's Armst

Worship came in many forms. So too did love and lust. For Aurélien Saint-Orlant, love and worship were devoutly displayed to the priest before him. Aurélien's heart swelled when he gazed upon the man behind the altar, his mind hazy from the overwhelming scent of frankincense and myrrh. He hung off of his every word, no matter if they were the words of the Lord or the tales of his youth, anything Father Celio said had an enthralling quality. Aurélien would listen to Father Celio speak the in-depth instructions on how to use a printing press if it meant hearing his voice for longer.

He thought about Julius, of all the corrupt, lustful deeds he wished to partake in with the prostitute. Rushing there after church was sinful, even for a man as riddled with Hellish thoughts as Lord Aurélien Saint-Orlant.

Time passed all too quickly, and Aurélien was beside himself when Father Celio's sermon ended. He wanted to stay, to request his guidance, but the air within The Church of Sanctuary was smothering. He needed to leave before his heart's desires overcame his own rational thoughts.

Aurélien stepped out of the safety of The Church of Sanctuary into the haze filled city. The typically bustling crowds had dwindled to nearly nothing, stray carriages rushing past to bring their patrons home in time for sup. A pair of lamplighters lit the tall cast iron lanterns that lined the streets, casting the cobblestone and brick in warm light to replace the setting sun. As he walked down the street towards his waiting carriage the pain began to return, a burrowing ache that made his vision turn white for the briefest of moments. Was this the pain the great stags felt come the end of spring? He almost wished, for all his pain, he would grow a gorgeous set of antlers. At least then his suffering would mean something.

A young man sat on the box of his carriage; face hidden by an old woolen hat with only a tuft of straw yellow hair peeking out from beneath. Even the twin black steeds that pulled it seemed to be asleep where they stood. Aurélien expected nothing less from Bram and could hardly blame the equine for sleeping. Though it may shine badly upon himself, he had been within the church for hours while the young man sat perched on the box awaiting his arrival. Aurélien tapped on the side of the carriage with the bottom of his walking stick, a beautiful piece of black lacquered wood topped with a silver dragon that twisted around the piece like a snake.

"Bram, has the cold stolen you?" Aurélien asked, situating himself into the carriage without the care to any detriment to his societal status that may cause.

A few thumps came from the box as Bram scrambled to make himself proper again. His voice was slightly muffled when he spoke, no thanks to the carriage between them and the knitted scarf Bram wore wrapped around his neck and mouth to shelter from the chill. "Where to, sir?"

Aurélien almost said home, but the reminder of Julius pulled at his loins. He could confess again when he saw Father Celio once more. The Lord was always forgiving of his sins, what was one more? Seeing Julius so soon after seeing Father Celio always made for an unforgettable night. "The Orchid House."

He Who Bleeds

✝✝✝

The Orchid House was situated in the depths of the city, a rather royal establishment for the debauchery that took place within. While it may be a brothel, it was the brothel to nobles—proudly boasting their history of serving princes and visiting kings as well as their ability to cater to any and every earthly desire a customer may possess. There was one keen element about The Orchid House that drew in their blue-blooded clientele: their ability to keep a secret. Discretion was practically woven into the very fabric of the sheets on the brothel's beds.

As Aurélien entered the gilded house decorated in the latest fashions from Paris, the sweet scent of smoke and liquor reached him before any of the perfumed beauties could. A woman in a striped, pink gown came to his side, the ruffles of her bustle dress scented heavily enough to make his head spin. Her chestnut brown hair had been pinned up with glass beads and silver. She pressed close to his side, smiling wide.

"Ah, Monsieur Saint-Orlant, how pleased we are to welcome you into our halls. It has been too long," she greeted, her French accent lingering on her words like dew on a leaf. With a curl of her finger two girls joined her in her crowding. They stripped him of his outer jacket, squirreling it off to safety.

"Madame Cecilia, lively as ever tonight I see. Is Julius available?" Aurélien asked as she guided him deeper into the building past gambling tables and women serving drinks to their wealthy patrons.

Madame Cecilia waved a hand. "Now Monsieur, I have told you a dozen times: we do not employ a Julius. Do you wish to rent a room or a service? One of our gorgeous gentlemen here would be glad to serve you or, if you desire a feminine charm, you know you have your pick of our ladies."

Aurélien furrowed his brows. Madame Cecilia always gave him the strangest of times when hiring Julius' services. He oft wondered if his beautiful Julius was a whore only for his enjoyment, a special exception a member of the house makes for him. Though he was only the second son of an inconsequential noble house—a pathetic little lordling who spent more time on his knees before Father Celio than creating anything worthwhile. At one point he had ambition to make a difference, to make something of himself beyond the expectation to care for his aging parent when the time came—beyond the title his father purchased for him. Beyond being a fraud. "A room would be nice. I always sleep better when I'm around others."

"Cost is the same as always, Monsieur Saint-Orlant, includes the company of one our best, if desired." Madame Cecilia reached into her pocket and produced a key. "Second door on the fourth floor, Monsieur."

He pressed two guineas into her palm in exchange for the key, bidding her goodnight before he made his way to his rented room. The room was as intricately decorated as the rest of the establishment, lodgings fit for a king. Upon the plush bed, lit by the warm light cast by the oil lamps and candles, was Julius. Aurélien stopped in the doorway, his breath caught in his lungs at the sight of him. It had been weeks since he had visited Julius and sought comfort within him, and meeting Julius by chance within Crockford's only resparked the desire to indulge in him.

Julius possessed a surreal beauty, one he could never forget, as if the image could ever fade from his mind. Despite

Julius' minute differences, Aurélien's perfect replacement for Father Celio lay right before him.

"I missed you, my love." Julius pouted as he slipped off the bed. He wore a cotton chiton to expose his delicate tanned limbs, the fabric clinging to what wasn't exposed. Julius wrapped his arms around Aurélien's neck.

"Did I keep you waiting long? We saw one another the other day." he asked, letting his hands fall to the small of Julius' back. Their bodies slotted together easily, well familiar with every inch of one another.

"A day apart is still far too long. What kept you away for so long?" As Julius spoke, his hands undid the buttons on his deep navy waistcoat, taking it away from him. He slipped away for a moment, laying the silk piece on a chest with a delicate hand.

"Oh, this and that. Spent most of this waking day within The Church of Sanctuary." Aurélien began undoing his own shirt until Julius returned to take over.

The smaller man stood on his toes, pressing their lips together hungrily. He tasted like the candied ginger Aurélien had gifted him during his last visit. "You spend an awful lot of time there, love."

"It is where I feel safe. Safe within, my mind calm. Father Celio keeps me grounded." Aurélien's words halted as thin fingers deftly removed the cravat and shirt from his body. The air was chill, but Julius' wandering hands on his chest were scorching, tracing over perked nipples while hungry lips chased his own.

"Talking about another man with me? Careful… I may get jealous." Julius nipped his bottom lip, drawing a moan from him.

"I can hardly help it, darling. I love him, but I can never have him. A man of the cloth… never to be mine… never to be possessed."

"Then possess me. Have me. What can a man of God offer that I can't?" Julius spoke with a steady cadence as if his hands didn't wander Aurélien's body, tracing scars and bruises without a care. The marred skin was sensitive, some fresh while others he had lived with as long as he had his strange condition. Those touches sent pleasant shivers right to his hardening cock. Julius looked up at him with an innocent expression that Aurélien couldn't refuse, dipping down to kiss his lover's plump lips.

He held the back of Julius' neck, keeping him in place while he tasted his lips. They were so soft against his own, licking into his mouth to taste more. Aurélien was lost entirely in Julius' warmth—the feel of his body against his own stirred his loins like no other.

"Let me buy your freedom, darling. Be mine. You refuse to tell me your debts. I will pay any, gladly, if you'll leave with me tonight," Aurélien pleaded against his lips.

Those words only made Julius giggle. Julius stepped away from him, making his way to the bed. He sat on the edge and spread his legs, making room for Aurélien to settle in between. He all but ran to him, finding a home between his thighs. "Please let me free you."

Julius reached up and cupped his cheek. "I am free, love. I am free with you."

"Julius… come home with me," he pleaded ever so sweetly. With a hand pressed to Julius' chest, he pushed him onto the bed. The soft sound slipping from his lips as he landed made Aurélien smile. As he crawled over him, he used his leg to further spread the other's. His hand rested on Julius' thigh, guiding his leg up so it may wrap around his waist.

"You may have me now, and in due time, for eternity. But for tonight, feast on my very soul as you see fit. I am yours for the taking until the sun tarnishes our beautiful night."

Aurélien hardly needed the pleas to claim what was his. He kissed Julius fiercely, filling it with every ounce of lust he felt for both Julius and for the true owner of his heart, Father Celio. They were both aware of what they were to one another. A replacement. A patron. Freedom. They found solace in one another's embrace like no other could.

Julius' hand slipped down, following a map of scars to the buttons of his trousers, undoing each with ease. Soft lips were on Aurélien's once more, ginger mingled with the taste of the Eucharist as their tongues toyed with one another. Sin and depravity unraveled the holy healing Aurélien spent so long obtaining. In a smooth motion he discarded the remains of his clothes, leaving him bare for Julius to defile.

"You are like a succubus," Aurélien complained, leaving his mark along the warm skin of Julius' neck. Something within him wanted to bite that tender flesh, to draw glorious blood and let it splatter and drip across the linens—and who was he to deny his urges? He bit.

Julius tossed his head back and moaned as Aurélien's canines sank into flesh, fragrant blood dripping onto his tongue like the most delicious fruit's juice. Tart like King Pine. He licked along the wound to sample more. Aurélien had held back of course, the small wounds only allowing pinpricks of blood to pool before it ceased bleeding. He wanted it to bleed. He wanted to feast on the slow death, but he remained restrained. For now.

"Something like that," Julius mused. He grabbed a fist full of hair and pulled Aurélien down into a hungry kiss. Between them he could feel Julius' erection, throbbing against his stomach. Aurélien became lost in his succubus' touches, his soul aflame. He rolled his hips against Julius, wanting some relief, more than just the loss of the aching pain in his head.

Julius pulled away from his lips, cheeks flushed, his breath hitched as tried to survive being devoured. "I believe it is time to get to work, my lord. Duty calls."

"Hmm?" Aurélien kissed along his neck, tasting the remnants of iron on his skin—delicious blood. "Why rush a good time? We have all night."

"Our celebratory sex can wait until after we win, Little Love." Julius' voice was deeper, horrifically familiar. Aurélien pulled away, sitting up only to lock eyes with the keeper of his heart.

Father Celio lay beneath him dressed in the same revealing chiton Julius had worn moments ago only now the garment was strained against the priest's muscles. He was as debauched as Julius had been, his pupils blown wide and his lips slick with their shared spit.

"F-Father Celio… what? How?"

"The *how* hardly matters. It's the *why* that brings in the money." Father Celio sat up and captured Aurélien's lips in a kiss, his forked tongue slipping into his mouth with ease. Aurélien sat as frozen as a marble statue as he was kissed, eyes wide. "Shall we go? Duke Isaac Cromwell is hardly going to bludgeon himself to death."

"Father Celio… I don't…"

Father Celio slipped off the bed, removing the chiton as he walked. He laughed at the call of his name. "Being called *Father* is rather amusing, you know? Still, I prefer daddy or Celio from your lips, Little Love."

Aurélien choked at the sight of Father Celio's bare form before him yet, despite how he willed it, he was unable to pull his eyes away.

"Now let us remove these ridiculous forms and be free as ourselves once more." Father Celio removed a simple black band from his finger, revealing a winged beast with horns jutting from the black tresses Aurélien longed to feel. A tail swished behind him, distracting his gaze for a moment. The man who he worshiped, the man who he praised as a god in place of the Catholic God was a demon. As beautiful as the demons within The Church of Sanctuary's paintings and windows. Self-portraits, he mused for the briefest of moments. It was as he gazed upon a demon with his own eyes that he remembered that demons were once angels. Even as a demon, Father Celio was angelic in a twisted fashion—his featherless wings plucked from an angel's into something reminiscent of a bat's, black leather fluttering with anticipation of flight. If Father Celio was handsome as a man, as a demon he was worth dying to please. Beautiful beyond compare, frighteningly so. How many had fallen to his charms?

Aurélien wished to join their ranks.

Father Celio reached towards him and, from his hand, removed the Saint-Orlant family's signet ring. "As much fun as it is to tease your human side, Au—I much prefer the demon within."

From his back tore wings, stretching wide in relief he didn't know he could feel. Horns burst forth from his temple, beads of blood birthed from the angry wounds. The pain was gone, even faster than it came. No longer did his skull throb or his bones ache. A demon burst forth from his own skin and, in the oddest way, he felt entirely unsurprised.

Waves upon waves of memories flooded back as the ring was removed from his finger and pressed into his hand. Lord Aurélien Saint-Orlant looked upon the demon and a demon looked back upon one of his own.

†Debt Collection†

A church bell rang twice in the distance. The witching hour would soon be upon them, and though it made Celio agitated and wired as he was forced to wait for the kill, Aurélien insisted on committing the act at 3 a.m., the time would make it far more poetic. His owner would be most pleased with their theatrics.

From their gargoyle perch upon a building across the way, they watched their target mingle about the gathering within his townhouse. He socialized about with others of his class, exchanging cup after cup of liquor with those who toasted their host, puffs and puffs of cigar smoke steamrolling from his face. He was a rather stout man, shorter than many of his peers, unknowingly turning many of them into shields of meat. There was very little of substance when it came to the person that was Duke Cromwell aside from an inherited title and the fortune he squandered away until his debts reached even the crown. Now as it stood, there was little use for the Cromwell name and the crown was hardly patient. His owner had, according to Celio, been all too excited to take up the order and pass it along to his chained demon.

Aurélien stretched his wings as he rolled his neck. Leaving the rich ladies and lordlings unscathed and none the wiser would be difficult—a rather exhilarating challenge to undertake. With a roll of his shoulders, his wings, which he had been so glad to release, returned to his body as did his horns. For some release, he allowed his tail to remain, wrapping it around his thigh beneath his frock.

"Let me remove the curse on that ring of yours. One snap and it's gone." Celio attempted to reach into his pocket to steal away the signet ring, hooking it with a claw.

"And what would I owe you? One hundred years of servitude?" Aurélien stole it back, tucking it once again into the safety of his pocket. "Besides, I thought you enjoyed riling up my boring human side. He's annoyingly in love with you."

"And you aren't, Little Love?" Celio tilted his head to the side. Aurélien rolled his eyes and waited patiently for a kiss. It landed on his cheek in seconds. "A century isn't all that long. Better to be owned by me than your rotten owner."

"I've worn your collar before, and while most exhilarating, I can't spend the next hundred years being your plaything. I don't have that kind of energy." Aurélien captured Celio's jaw, pulling him in for a more proper exchange. His sharp canines pricked the other demon's lips, tinting their mouths with beautiful red. "I have another decade at most under my master's control. I can wait. Just a pathetic human—old, frail, and smelling of piss."

"Gross." Celio's nose scrunched up. "Let's get this over with then, shall we?"

Aurélien nodded and stepped off the edge of the building, his wings slipped out to slow his descent before hiding away like they were never there. Celio landed beside him, shaping himself with the use of his ring into Julius once more—Father Celio was too well known of a figure to be seen at such a soirée.

The merchant's entrance was the ideal entryway for their uses—separate from the servants without the grandeur of the front entrance. Guided only by moonlight, Celio plucked a pick from his pocket and worked with relative quickness to open the lock, the door opening in mere seconds.

"A kiss for a job well done?" He blocked the doorway, pursing his lips.

"When the job is done perhaps." Aurélien pushed him aside and sauntered in. As he walked, fixing his ensemble as he went, Celio joined him at his side, hooking an arm with his.

"Cromwell is to be beaten for his assets. If he does not comply, they will be taken after death by the crown. The messier the better, honestly."

"Oh, you do know how to excite me." Aurélien grinned, opening the door that would lead to the soirée. The prospect of delicious torture along with the boring old hunt excited him in a way he could scant describe.

Few guests turned their gaze to them as they entered and, with practiced ease, they slipped into the fray. Aurélien was acquainted with many in attendance so slinking in was easier than most of their jobs.

Lady Anna Polle, whose grandfather was eighth in line for the throne, welcomed him with open arms to the soirée and her chatty nature pushed away any questions others may have about their oddly late entrance. Aurélien sipped on white wine, occasionally stealing looks at his target. He didn't expect Cromwell to have a single inkling that assassins were out for him let alone demons from the fiery pits of Hell, but he'd much rather not interrupt his target's writhing upon some poor woman.

While enjoying a surprisingly interesting conversation with Lady Polle about the current fashions in Paris and the rise of machine-made lace, Celio tugged on the end of his tail. He stood on his toes and whispered to Aurélien, his lips ghosting over the lobe of his pointed ear. "I'll set him up for you, Little Love. Find us soon."

Aurélien watched as Celio walked away towards their target, his form taking on the sway of a woman's as he changed his shape once more. He'd stay in idle conversation while he waited, telling fanciful stories to delight Lady Polle and the others, who were of little to no consequence. After waiting ample time, Aurélien slipped away, excused himself for the night, and found his way through the winding halls to Celio's side once more.

His little false priest had set up within the master bedroom, still disguised as a woman. Celio had straddled their target, her breasts bare and pressed against his chest while she kissed him with slow movements. The door closing behind him caused Cromwell to stop.

Aurélien strode across the room and grabbed a large wardrobe. With ease he pushed it in front of the only exit. It hardly made a sound as it moved, no more than a shoe scuffing on the hardwood would.

"Having fun without me?" Aurélien asked, rolling his shoulders as his wings and horns reappeared.

Cromwell's scream was silenced by Celio's hand clasping over his mouth. A second muffled scream came from their target as Celio shifted back into his devilishly handsome form.

"Not too much fun. He's small and can't kiss for shit." Celio pouted, slinking around Cromwell. With a single hand he dragged him off the bed and strapped him to a plush chair using golden decorative rope from the curtains. He plucked a handkerchief from Cromwell's pocket and stuffed it into his mouth.

He Who Bleeds

"Nobody said you had to kiss him," Aurélien remarked, conjuring his bag of tools from his personal void. He caught it before it fell, setting it down on the bed. Inside were his favorite items—iron rods, scalpels, butcher's blades, pliers, and anything else he could need. "Celio, how much does he owe exactly?"

"If you let me take care of that binding ring you'd know these things. I wouldn't have to parrot information from your owner to you. Heavens above, you wouldn't even have an owner if I broke it."

"Section 17 of the infernal contract: *the demon spawn cannot possess knowledge of their owner's identity*. Section 27, Clause E: *destruction of the contractee will result in the destruction of both the contractee and contractor*. Ergo, I will perish if you break my contract. My contract ends when either the contractee or the contractor dies on the mortal plane. You know this." Aurélien plucked a pair of pliers from his bag. This was one of his favorite methods. The removal of teeth and nails never killed but the pain was enough to make someone talk. "How much, Celio?"

Celio groaned. "Something like… ten thousand? Too much honestly. Think about what my little church could do with that kind of money."

"You'd use it to buy more excitement for your dungeon," Aurélien commented. He stood before Cromwell now. "I'm going to remove your gag now. Cry for help and you'll be without a tongue before you can get a word out."

Muffled words came from their target.

Aurélien rolled his eyes. "Nod your head if you agree."

Cromwell nodded his head bnd Aurélien removed the gag. Celio stood behind the human, clawed fingers dancing over his shoulders and neck to keep him in line. It hardly mattered to either of them if the money was found, but the excitement of torture was too much to pass up. With each of their contracts preventing the harm of humans outside of their missions, fun had to be had when allowed.

"Please, please, whatever you want you can have. Just let me go!" Cromwell begged, voice quivering as much as he sniveled pathetically.

Looking down at Cromwell, Aurélien's lip curled in disgust. "You've got a bounty on your head, no small one either. Begging isn't going to do you any good."

"I can pay! Please… just let me go. I need a few weeks to pull the money together, but I can—"

"Payment tonight in *full*." Celio purred, his hands wrapping around Cromwell's neck. One of his claws sliced into his skin as their target jerked his head to the side. Aurélien watched the trickle of blood flow down his skin like he was in a trance. Beautiful ruby red rivulets of blood. Celio had to snap his fingers twice to gain his attention.

"Let's begin." Aurélien drew his eyes away from the blood. Ever since Aurélien learned, at least in the darkness of night, of his true nature, he had been plagued with a lust for blood. The blood from this pathetic, worthless man only ignited the fires within. The very sight of it aroused him like nothing else.

"I don't know what you want."

Aurélien hummed, then punched their target. Celio held the chair still, grinning as he watched. Broken sobs echoed in the otherwise quiet room from the man who had never had a hand raised to him aside from childhood spankings.

"We are here to collect, Cromwell. Ten thousand pounds sterling, gold, shillings. However you wish to pay, we accept. So… tell us where the money is."

"I-I don't have… the money," Cromwell spat.

Celio draped himself over the human from behind, trailing his claws over the man's cheeks. "You might want to tell him where to find the money. Be good and you'll leave with only a few bruises and a missing finger."

"Missing finger?" His question was punctuated with a scream, muffled by Celio's quick hand.

"Missing finger," Aurélien repeated, holding the finger up to the light to watch the ring it wore sparkle. Blood fell from the wound onto the hardwood floors in fat drops, the scent filling Aurélien's mind with near ecstasy.

Cromwell grit his teeth, trying to bear the pain while Aurélien pondered his next step. He was well aware he was too quick to take his prize, but it had been weeks since he had the pleasure of coating his hands with the grime of a human's innards. A lower demon would place the finger in their mouth, run their tongue around the wound and suck the marrow from the bones— there was once a time when Aurélien would have done the same. Now, however, he was practiced. He knew how to savor the experience. Strip the skin and meat from the bone and arrange the little bones in his box of trophies—which Celio was kind enough to keep for him, lest his human side find it within his chambers.

"Let's try that again. Where's the money? They can either find a… mostly intact corpse or one with many, many missing parts." Aurélien thought about the scene he would paint. Perhaps they'd only find his head, maybe even just a single eye placed on a pile of bills, the rest of his putrid sinew scorched away by infernal flames. The glee and excitement at the mere fantasy made him grin. "I'm not a very patient demon, Cromwell, and my owner is even less."

"Fuck you," Cromwell spat, his spittle only traveling as far as his chin.

Celio laughed, dragging the man's head back by the hair to look at him. His long dark hair slipped over his shoulders creating a curtain around Cromwell. Even for a devil, Celio was otherworldly handsome, so much so that Aurélien was often in awe of his beauty. Even more so when he was lavished in love from the bothersome incubus. Purring, Celio teased, "That's my job."

"Now how would you like to do this? What's painful for you, ah—makes wonderful fun for us."

"Mhm, Au is wonderful with a knife. He could turn your insides out without you bleeding dry. I once saw him feed a man his own beating heart." Celio swooned, sighing in bliss. He slipped away from Cromwell to dance his hands across Aurélien's chest. "Can you imagine that? Dying to your own teeth! He's so inventive."

"You will both burn in Hell for this! Homosexual creatures of Hell out for the blood of a good Christian man! What are you being paid? I'll double it. I'll triple it! Just let me go… take my family… take anything you want but let me live! I must live. I need to live. Damn you, damn you all to Hell! O' God, save your loyal servant."

Celio let out an exasperated sigh. He conjured a book of bound parchment and a pen, filled with details on their hundreds of targets. He spoke out loud as he wrote. "Target Duke Isaac Cromwell was uncooperative. Assets to be seized by debtors. Left ring finger taken as token. Death by… Little Love, what do you plan to do? Ah, I'll just fill it in later… I can see you're about to disregard all of our work here."

Pleading. Such pathetic pleading. They all spoke those words when the reality of their situation set in. Only the worst ever offered their family in exchange and those in particular always sucked the joy from Aurélien in an odd way. Something lost from his own sordid history, locked away due to his contract no doubt. He cared not for the details, only the punishment for uttering such words. Anger always replaced that joy. The mission became inconsequential. Only death would soothe him.

"So selfish…" Aurélien muttered, picking up a scalpel from his array of tools. He looked to Celio who gladly steadied their target, grasping his head on either side. "They'll be glad to be rid of you."

Ugly reddened eyes bulged from Cromwell's head; his breath heavy to the point of slobbering with the force he used to thrash about against the bindings. All that effort did little but amuse Celio.

The scalpel was one of Aurélien's favorite tools. Naturally, it couldn't wield the power a knife did, but the precision well made up for its size. He could easily play with his target for hours without them dying, easily remove pieces and parts he wished to discard to create his masterpieces. Luckily for Cromwell, it slid so easily into the soft meat of his right eye. It made a wet sound like when sliding a knife into a jar of delicious apple preserves, and much like Aurélien did with his preserves, he twisted the scalpel about in the eye socket until it was perfectly ruined and turned into a jelly-like paste. Even through the handkerchief that Celio stuffed into his mouth, Cromwell screamed so beautifully. So perfectly. A symphony of his own creation to rival even the works of Mozart. Glee replaced his anger, the thrill of the act soothing his whole being.

As far as Aurélien was concerned, there was no better feeling than performing for an audience—and Celio was most reactive, grinning as he held Cromwell's body in place, shaking with his own excitement at the carnage.

"Ah! What a beautiful mess."

"It's art," Aurélien muttered, already losing his excitement. What would be next? He could remove his bowels, string him from the canopy of his bed using those twisting intestines—allow him to slowly bleed to death. The very idea was exciting and he thought no longer of other potential methods. Was it far too much for retribution over late payments? Naturally, but so was hiring the services of a demon. One would not expect a demon to handle matters in a human way, it simply was not in their nature. Aurélien's scalpel sliced through the clothing hiding Cromwell's flesh from him. Wool and linen sliced away easily under his blade, much like his skin would soon. Wistfully he informed Celio of his plans. His little incubus would no doubt love the idea. "I want to string him up… hang him by his innards like one of those circus acts."

"That will be beautiful, Little Love," Celio praised. He conjured his book again and finished his previous thoughts. "Duke Isaac Cromwell was disemboweled and suspended via the intestines. Right eye was… removed. Left to perish via blood loss."

The press of a scalpel against quivering flesh was nothing short of exhilarating. Blood escaped the wound like a flood, and as to not damage his precise work, he ignored the screaming and writhing from his unwilling participant as best as he could.

Beautiful art required pain and Cromwell would just have to learn that the hard way it seemed.

Celio watched with rapt attention, cooing his delight and adornment to Aurélien as the blade cut through flesh, fat, and meat to expose pulsing, twisting intestines. The target had become silent and only the heaving, gasping breaths he took assured Aurélien that he was very much alive. Sniveling, pathetic, worthless—but alive. Celio bounced on his heels, full of energy now that his hands were no longer occupied with silencing Cromwell.

"I should do my rounds, Little Love. Try not to kill him while I'm gone." Celio stretched his arms above his head, standing on his toes to crack everything he could before shifting into the form of Duke Isaac Cromwell. Looking upon his beautiful incubus turned into a disgusting man made Aurélien's skin crawl in a way no amount of gore and carnage could. Celio came to kiss his cheek and Aurélien had to dodge his lips. The incubus laughed and slipped through the darkness to keep up the show that Duke Cromwell was alive and well, at least for now.

Clawed fingers slipped into the abdominal cavity, pulling the intestines from Cromwell like a candymaker pulling taffy. It fell in a heap onto the floor, staining Aurélien's fingers with the juices of a doomed fellow. As the room succumbed to the overwhelming scent of iron, Aurélien felt alive again. More himself—freer than he had been in months. This act was not one demanded by his owner; this was entirely for himself. The hours in which he was in control of himself were few and far between, always trapped within the anxious, disgustingly in love human that was himself.

Aurélien hummed as he began his art. A large canopy bed made of carved oak stood proudly in the room, and with the curtains disposed of, he had the perfect place to suspend the man. The result was worth the effort. Beauty didn't even begin to cover the pure glory that was his art. His devotion to the dark. Cromwell heaved breaths as he hung in the air, suspended by the limbs using his still pulsing innards. He hoped Celio returned from his mingling to see his unholy creation before the subject died. It wouldn't be as wonderful to see if that chest ceased rising and falling.

He didn't know how long he spent feeling the organs of his prey between his fingers, admiring his handiwork but the arms wrapping around his waist told him enough had passed.

"It's magnificent, Little Love. Some of your best work," he praised, leaving kisses along the exposed skin of his neck. Cromwell gurgled on his own blood above them. "Let's go home, okay?"

"Mm… will my owner be pleased with this?"

Celio thought for a moment, walking his way before Aurélien pulled him into his arms. "Not at all, he would've liked to handle this discreetly, but he should know your habits by now. But I like it. You're skilled, nothing short of a master craftsman!"

"A sweet thing talking sweeter words." Aurélien ran two blood-stained fingers along Celio's throat, feeling the quickened pulse beneath the pads of his fingertips. Celio purred, pressing himself closer to him, the air between them burned like the very fires of Hell.

"The truth can be as sweet as me on occasion." Their lips met with more bite than an imp. Aurélien wouldn't use *love* to describe how he felt for Celio. It transcended that emotion. For as long as he could remember Celio had been by his side—his Hellsent incubus who tended to him with as much grace as a palace harlot. He couldn't imagine a life without Celio, they completed each other as though forged in Hellfire from the same mold. Word of his affection for the bothersome man certainly reached to the heavenly scourge his human side prayed to each day. Celio was his weakness, and he didn't care who or what knew. "Ravish me, Little Love, we have celebrating to do."

"Darling, you hardly have to ask."

Aurélien's back hit the plush mattress and he hardly had the time to sit up before Celio was upon him, desperate hands tearing at his clothes until they were both bare as the day they were created. Celio's wings shrouded them much like the waterfall of black hair did, the blood dripping from Cromwell's pathetic form falling around them like rain. He cupped Aurélien's cheeks in his hands and kissed him like he starved. He very well may be, it had been weeks since they sought succor in one another's body— weeks since Celio had fed on his body.

Tongues pressed against one another in a slow dance as their hands wandered one another's forms. Aurélien's hands found pleasure in roaming the plump ass of the incubus, earning him anticipatory sounds and pleased little moans falling from Celio's lips. His silly little lover was already hard, his cock pressed between them—smearing his mess between their stomachs with each needy roll of his hips.

"Needy." Aurélien clicked his tongue, slapping the round rear he loved so much. He soothed the pain by rubbing small circles around the base of the other's tail. "Have I been letting you starve?"

Celio whined, choked off moans on his tongue. "You've been abusing me, Little Love—I'm starving. I need you, I want you. All of you."

"Then have me." It was a taunt and Celio rose to the challenge. His incubus was insatiable, something Aurélien learned long ago. Hungry didn't begin to cover what Celio was and Aurélien, in all of his kindness, would do anything to satiate his desires.

A strong hand was placed on his bicep, pinning him down onto the bed, as though Aurélien would ever fight back against being made into a meal. Celio was talented—being skilled was in his nature, but it never ceased to surprise, and occasionally embarrass, Aurélien with how easily he stirred in his touch.

"I'll be called upon tomorrow to say prayers for your recovery, won't I?" Celio asked, stroking his cock in slow rhythmic motions, smearing his beading precum along his shaft.

A moan slipped from his throat, Celio's lips on his. Devouring him until he could only gasp out his words. When he was given a breath of air, Celio's mouth found his neck. "Mmmnn—you claim to be starving yet tease me so."

Celio hummed, licking his way up to his ear, nibbling on the lobe. "I'm still deciding how I want you."

"Why question it? I know you want me deep inside you— to feel how you make it throb." Aurélien's fingers twisted up in Celio's dark hair, guiding him to his lips again. He was keenly aware that Celio loved the tingle of pain, his hushed little whimpers solidifying that fact once more. They kissed open mouthed, licking into each other's maws, their desire overpowering all thought but the here and now. "Won't you show me how good you are at taking me? How well you can ride... oh, I know you'll look beautiful quivering around my cock."

"You know how to rile me up, Little Love." He breathed a sigh drenched in ecstasy. Celio straddled Aurélien properly, sitting up as proudly as his cock did. Nipples pebbled and cheeks flushed with anticipation, a most glorious sight. Cromwell hung above them like a fiendish canopy, dripping blood onto their bodies. It smeared across their skin like hot oil. Aurélien could hardly name a wonder more deserving of worship than the incubus before him. With practiced ease Celio summoned a salve into his hand and drenched his cock with the musk scented grease.

Aurélien savored every touch with reverence, daring to reach up and cup his cheek. "I am in awe of you."

A giggle and Celio pressed into his hand like a feline receiving a pet. "Sweet words won't make me go faster."

"Do you blame me for trying?"

The demon bit his palm, not hard enough to cause pain—quite the opposite in fact. A low growl came from Aurélien, rolling his hips to gain even an ounce of relief.

"Shh, Little Love, one does not rush to devour a feast such as yourself. It must be savored. Tasted with the skill of a sommelier. My lust for you burns hotter than Hellfire, I must temper the flames lest I burn thine flesh." Celio dipped down, rewarding him with a kiss. Incubus spit was an addictive substance—an aphrodisiac more effective than a spread of fig and pomegranate, though saliva from an incubus was not nearly as effective as their semen. It seeped into his mind with every messy kiss they exchanged, loosening his grip on reality. Aurélien oft craved it as much as Celio did, though his devilish lover informed him quite often that the effects were not enough to create desire from nothing. What they possessed went far beyond the addiction found in opium dens.

Teeth grazed along the thin skin stretched over his jugular, so easily bitten out yet, instead of welcomed bloodshed, marks were left. Deep splotchy marks that would remain well into the next day and most certainly the day following it. His human self would blush and stammer at the sight. Would he take himself in hand and attempt to remember the night? Would he dream of Father Celio's lips upon his flesh, unaware of how true those fantasies were? Would he fuck up into his too tight grip and pretending it was a godly man's tight and inviting hole? He would probably even place money on the possibility that his human self's fantasy would simply be the priest's hand upon his cock. If only his human self could see that the fantasy was no mere dream. That his wildest desires were mere foreplay to them.

Celio, ever skilled as he was, brought him to near completion over and over, his hands leaving his body until the ecstasy within Aurélien's veins slipped away. It was during those times he worked himself open, making little whimpers to entice Aurélien even more. If Celio had not trained him so well over the years he would have pounced when the first whine left the incubus' lips. The show was done with carefully practiced elegance, done in view of his willing victim. Fingers dipped inside Celio's tight hole, and he howled with pleasure as fingers curled within. His eyes never left Aurélien's, as if to taunt him. Aurélien's hands rested on the incubus' strong thighs, feeling the muscles flex as the other worked himself up, grinding on the three fingers buried inside.

"Do you even need me here?" Aurélien asked, trailing his hands up to his hips. "Not that I don't enjoy the show."

"Patience," Celio chided, biting his bottom lip to keep his cry of pleasure silent.

Aurélien reached up, grabbing him by the scruff and pulling him down into a crushing, needy kiss. Celio took both of their cocks in hand, rolling his hips.

"I can't be patient anymore. I need you—don't you want to feed?" Aurélien broke their kiss, his breath heavy. His incubus looked down at him with half lidded eyes.

Celio pressed his hands flat onto his chest, pushing him down onto the plush bedding. "I don't need to fuck to feed."

"Mhm, but isn't it better to feast rather than sample? Indulge yourself. Leave your mark on me. I will gladly give all that you need."

"Ah, you're so sweet for me." Celio leaned down, licking away the fresh blood speckling his chest. "Say please."

Aurélien was no stronger than any other man, demonic nature aside. He wanted relief, pleasure—ecstasy beyond what mere mortals can possess, and his Celio could provide. "Please."

"Good boy." With ease he took Aurélien's cock in hand and sank down onto his erection. Aurélien moaned, resisting fucking up into the other's tight heat. Celio enjoyed taking the lead, even when riding him like the most skilled equestrian.

Long ink black hair slipped over Celio's shoulders as he worked himself to bliss on Aurélien's cock, shrouding his face in curtains. Feeding for an incubus was a ritual of the utmost depravity. Behind him his tail flicked about, swishing against Aurélien's legs and the bed in excitement. Aurélien's hands were not nearly as still as his hands, trailing up Celio's strong chest.

Any thoughts of teasing the Hellsent man were quickly forgotten as Celio cried out in pleasure, tossing his head back. His movements halted.

"Let me take care of you," Aurélien offered, taking it upon himself to pin Celio into the mattress. His tail wrapped itself around Celio's. Looking down at Celio was even more enjoyable than looking up at him. The false priest looked at him with half-lidded eyes, his breath hitched, and lips wet with their shared saliva. Depraved and sinful. Aurélien kissed him until he whined, rolling his hips to keep their lust aflame. His release was too imminent and the fear of finishing within his lover too soon kept his desire to claim at bay.

The muffled moans from Celio spoke of his own skills, despite being far from an incubus like the other. With each slow rock of his hips, he clearly brushed against that bud of pleasure within. There was a certain pride in making a mess of a demon of sex and pleasure—and Aurélien rivaled Hybris with his ego in that regard. Only his skills with a blade came close to being a source of pride.

"The last thing he'll hear is your delicious pleas." Aurélien mouthed his mark along Celio's neck, marks so high not even his vestments would hide his sins. Would it make his human self jealous? Would he rise to the challenge? What a naughty boy his human self would be when he saw them. Surely jealousy would plague him, turning him more demonic than any set of horns and wings could ever do. That knowledge only spurred his desire to claim Celio more—inside and out.

"Mh! Let him hear. He should thank us for bathing—ah— in his blood!" Celio laughed, throwing back his head in pleasure. His claws dragged down Aurélien's back, cutting deep enough to draw blood and add to the myriad of scars lining his body. It ran hot, mixing with the sprinkling from above that hit his unholy flesh.

Aurélien nipped at his lips before praising his lover. His thrusts began to become more desperate as he neared his own completion. "That's it, good little priest."

"Human you—nnnh—he'll be so jealous!" Nails dug into his flesh again as he fucked into the tight heat. Celio's hole squeezed around his throbbing cock, milking him to completion. An incubus' aphrodisiac, the thrill of creating bloody art and the pure pleasure of fucking his lover made for a far quicker act than he would have desired. A few hard rough thrusts had him spilling into Celio's hole, the other cumming with a couple skilled jerks of his hand.

Celio cried out as he finished, his eyes glowing an otherworldly gold as he finally fed. Aurélien marked along the column of his throat, rolling his hips slowly as they both came down from their collective high. This was their covenant. Assistance for relief. It had changed over the years, warped in odd ways, but they held no official contract between one another. When they became their only lovers neither could say but Aurélien was nothing but pleased to pick up the slack when it came to feeding the insatiable incubus beneath him. Already, just moments after he pulled out and caught his breath did the pest grin up at him and demand another helping.

"You may always remove my binding ring and feast when you desire," Aurélien reminded, slicking back his sweat damp hair.

"Mh, I know but the reward tastes better when I'm starving. A feast is not a feast when one indulges in gluttony each day." Celio collected his clothing from the floor, shrugging on each layer as he spoke.

"One day you'll become so hungry you jump my human self. He'll die the second you kiss him."

Julius stood before Aurélien again, reaching delicate fingers up to fasten his cravat back into place. "I love teasing human you. He just about died today! Slipped off my glamours a little early to see that confused little face. You get this furrow between your brows—oh, just like that."

Aurélien's brows did in fact furrow, not just in confusion, but fear as well. If his human self saw, if he saw everything, it would be disastrous. Such knowledge didn't go against the contract but verged close to Section 4, Clause B: *contractor must keep a clean presence within high society.* If his human self acted irrationally, it could all come crashing down within an instant. "You did *what?*"

"What's the big deal, it was only a glimpse."

"The big deal he asks!" Aurélien scoffed, raking a hand over his face. "He cannot know about anything that happens. He needs to remain oblivious! If he knows, he will question everything. *Everything.* If the Yard ever connects what we do here to him, he has deniability, you can't—"

The door handle to the master suite rattled and a woman's sweet voice came from the other side. "Sweetie?"

"Let's talk about this later," Aurélien whispered, taking one last look around the room. He threw open a window and he, along with Celio, made a speedy escape from the scene of the crime.

†Wretchedness†

Pain bloomed across his body, swallowing his mind in throbbing agony worse than the morning after a drunken night. The curtains within his room were drawn, blocking out much of the late morning sun. His bed was warm, the blankets bunched up as though he had not been the sole occupant. Aurélien sighed and pushed himself up, pressing the palm of his hand to the throbbing points of his skull. He long since ceased questioning how he arrived home after such strange nights. Whatever happened was a mystery—there was no use dwelling on the unknown.

Slipping out of bed, he tugged on his housecoat, the warmth providing him with some meager comfort. Aurélien pulled a rope from beside his bed to summon his valet and set himself to open the blinds. Outside, London was alive, the city bustling as the social season began. Like migrating birds, those with heavy pockets flocked to the city for the season, crowding Knightsbridge with their influx. Theia had written some odd days ago to inform him of her intentions to darken his doorstep in the coming weeks. She'd be arriving soon, and if she didn't, he'd have to craft a telegram and inquire on her health.

"You rang, sir?" asked his valet, a slim stick of a man with ash-blond hair and a square jaw that Aurélien found most agreeable. Aurélien felt a sense of pride when it came to his valet, he had been in his care since they were both youths—Oscar, a stable boy plucked from the stalls to attend to a young Aurélien's needs. They were as thick as thieves, and despite often assurance from Aurélien that such formality between old friends was hardly necessary, Oscar insisted on it—at least until his workday was over and he happily returned to calling Aurélien all manner of names.

"A bath, Oscar."

"Dorcas already has the water heating, sir." Oscar swept past him and properly opened the blinds and windows. He placed the latest issue of *The Illustrated London News* and a copy of the morning broadsheet on the small table within the room. "Do you require anything else?"

"Coffee and something for this ache."

A curt bow of the head. "Of course, sir."

"Do you know when I arrived home? Haven't the faintest clue."

"As always you were as quiet as a mouse upon your return. I suspect it must have been late, I was up rather late and didn't hear a sound."

Aurélien sighed and waved Oscar off. The magazine was dull, yet he devoured the contents, hardly noticing the arrival of Oscar with coffee, a small breakfast and laudanum for the pain—an old friend that soothed all his worries. He ate and drank in relative silence, flipping through his magazine mostly to admire the artwork inside. He cared not for the often prattling words inside and he hadn't enough mind left to pick through the writing within to fully understand, not with sleep still clinging to him the same way the ache in his skull did. The laudanum didn't work fast enough for his liking and Aurélien gave up on reading the broadsheet as the last dregs of coffee were swallowed down. A hot bath was in order.

The washroom was sweltering with the steam rolling off the waiting bath water and he was made to wipe the mirror with the sleeve of his robe in order to shave. A man of his status would often allow his servants to wield the blade, but there were certain things Aurélien preferred to do himself—there was something rather unsettling to him about baring the most vulnerable part of one's body to a blade within another's hand. A queer sort of worry, but a worry, nevertheless. He had no doubts that Oscar was entirely loyal to him and murdering his employer was, at the very least, rarely on his mind.

Aurélien stripped and spent a moment searching for the marks causing him such dull throbbing pain. His neck and chest were a mess of bruises, claiming marks dotted about without a care to who may see. These didn't ache, superficial bruises that'd fade in a week's time. What ached were the various cuts across his chest and back like he had been clawed by a wild animal. The flesh was red and raw, but clean with not a speck of dried blood to be found. As he gently poked and prodded at the meat, the wounds began to ooze pinpricks of blood again. He pressed a linen cloth to them, dabbing away the blood until the cloth turned a mess of pink and red smears.

The water was a long-awaited welcome, the hot steam engulfing him as much as the near scalding liquid did. Aurélien rested against the porcelain, letting the water ease the ache in his body. What had he got himself into last night? These wounds could hardly be made by the delicate Julius. As he relaxed, Aurélien tried to piece together the night as best as he remembered.

What he could parse together was nothing special— visiting The Orchid House and requesting Julius, playing along with Madame Cecilia's same jest about him not existing and proving her wrong upon entering the rented room. Naturally, he remembered his moments with Julius well. How beautiful he looked beneath him, the taste of his lips against his, the feel of their bodies together. Such bliss. He almost wished he could run for The Orchid House again and, if he had been a man with a lower status in society, he may very well have done so.

The more he reminisced on the night before the stranger the memories became. Aurélien almost laughed at his own foolish imagination. For what he remembered was pure fantasy. It had been Father Celio beneath him. Kind, godly, perfect Father Celio. His lips were the ones that tasted so sweet. The very thought stirred his loins. He could push them aside with ease, if he wanted—but he dared not. Aurélien allowed his mind to linger on the faux memory.

Tasting ginger on his tongue, feeling strong hands trace the scars lining his body. Would his touch bless him? Heal the wounds buried deep within? Would he finally be saved from the missing nights and blurred memories if Father Celio truly touched him? Aurélien stroked himself with a tight, quick movement of his hand, his mind plagued with flashes beyond his typical imagination. Father Celio, horned and winged like a demon, sat upon him, riding him like the unholiest of beings. He could almost feel it— the wet heat, the feeling of the priest's claws on his flesh. Devious thoughts that led to him cumming into his hand at the most pathetic speed.

His nose scrunched up at the mess he made, stepping out of the bath. With a pull to the plug, his shame disappeared. As he dressed himself in wool twill garments with carefully polished silver buttons, his mind wandered to Father Celio once more. He needed to see his messiah, beg for forgiveness for such horrific thoughts. Depraved thoughts regarding his most holy, virginal form.

He would repent. Forsake his worldly possessions if he must. Aurélien brushed past his valet as he left his rooms, hair still damp. He only paused to be assisted into a frock coat and presented a hat and cane.

"Shall I call for a carriage, sir?" Oscar asked, well aware of his employer's predicament. After all, Aurélien had been storming off to The Church of Sanctuary nearly every morning for as long as either could remember.

"I'll go by foot today."

✝✝✝

Sermons had always been a dull affair before Father Celio came into Aurélien's life as the object of his worship. Imbecilic, wearisome speeches read aloud from a musty book that held neither his hope nor his interest. Paired with the sagged, ugly faces of the priests—their monotonous, dragging voices aside—Aurélien would rather burn for eternity than sit for one more moment within their cursed churches. Perhaps if their sermons were anything but drab, Aurélien wouldn't have felt as though he was a creature of Hell on holy soil within their establishments.

Father Celio and The Church of Sanctuary, however, were different. Beautiful and charming were words that only scraped the surface of how Aurélien viewed the holy man. He wished to write poetry about his beauty and craft novels in regard to his golden eyes. Aurélien knew in his heart that there was no sin greater than loving another man, yet his soul ached at the mere thought of tamping it down. If Mass was the only respite from his longing, Aurélien would attend each one and hang from those spoken words like spiders from silk.

More often than not, Aurélien found himself nodding along to Father Celio's preaching, the words losing all meaning as he became nearly hypnotized by the fluttering of the priest's lashes. That particular morning was no different, Aurélien completely transfixed on the sway of the priest's braid. He wondered if it too would smell like the incense burned in the church or if it held the sweet smell of perfume. Aurélien considered purchasing a perfume for the man—handcrafted and as refined as the priest himself. If he did, would Father Celio accept it? Would he wear such a material thing as a godly man? Even if the priest refused, Aurélien decided he would gift him thusly.

With such desires came the return of far more perverse inclinations. Aurélien watched the movement of Father Celio's hands and wished to bite the tips of his fingers—not enough to draw blood, but breathy gasps. He wanted to kiss up his arm, rend the priest from his vestments, and press him against the Lord's altar. Father Celio would have a rather sensitive neck, Aurélien concluded, and he wanted nothing more than to mouth along it, leaving marks wherever his lips went.

Mass ended rather abruptly, in Aurélien's opinion. Though this mattered little when he spent a majority of it daydreaming about fragrances he wished to smell on onyx hair and where he wished to mark the priest.

Aurélien all but rushed into the confessional following morning Mass. The dimly lit wicker booth was safe and secluded—as though mahogany and weaved reeds could hold back the demons flooding his mind.

He Who Bleeds

The door beside him opened and closed, a small sigh leaving the holy man's mouth. Though hazed through the wicker, Aurélien knew the man who sat opposite him was not Father Celio. "Get out."

"Pardon?" Deacon Wren asked, as if Aurélien had been anything but clear.

"I will not confess to you. Leave me. I wish to see Father Celio."

"Father Celio is indisposed, at present. I promise I can assist you in your confessions, my child."

Aurélien swallowed down his rising anger. He knew, logically, that Deacon Wren had done no wrong, yet it did little to sooth his jealousy and hurt. "Please. Tell him it is Aurélien who requires his ear. He knows… he knows the right thing to say."

Deacon Wren muttered under his breath and left the confessional.

Minutes passed before Father Celio entered the booth, the scent of frankincense following him. "Forgive me, my child. I've kept you waiting."

"Father Celio…"

"Yes, my child?"

Aurélien only said his name again, mournfully. Tears pricked at the corners of his eyes. "Father Celio…"

"I am here, Lord Saint-Orlant."

"Father Celio, please… how do I stop the pain? How do I stop these dreams, these nightmares? I cannot spend my life in this agony anymore."

"All is healed in the eyes of the true Lord." Father Celio opened his Bible, the parchment pages turning with a crinkle between his gentle fingers. "All is healed if you pray for it."

"Anything. I'd give anything, Father Celio." Aurélien breathed out slowly, hoping to regulate the overflowing emotions he felt. "Forgive me, Father, for I have sinned. It has been mere days since my last confession and I am drenched in sin."

"Let us pray, my lost lamb. We will pray for your freedom—for your rebirth. With luck, it shall happen before the week's end."

†Terminus†

The Church of Sanctuary accepted him into its gaping maw, a familiar beast within his routine. The old wooden doors, ones nearly as ancient as Charlemagne's rule, groaned under their own weight. To Aurélien's relief, the noise of his entrance didn't disrupt the service. With quickness he sat himself in a center pew, alone and as close to the ever-beautiful Father Celio as he dared to be when so coated in sin.

His priest looked serene as he spoke the word of the Lord in his well-practiced tongue, but it was not the words spoken that Aurélien found himself enthralled with. With a tight braid of black hair draped teasingly over his blood red cope, Father Celio wore his typical cassocks and pellegrina—a garment embroidered with gold spun thread with such precision that it seemed to shine in the candlelight, hypnotizing the lord more than any prayer could.

Those prayers fell on partially deaf ears—ones which only heard the deep rumble of Father Celio's voice echoing in the nearly empty church. It stirred something in him, not tears or joyous worship, but ungodly desire for the man preaching before him. Father Celio's eyes were on him, as though he were speaking only to him. Praying for only him. His alone. Taunting. His.

With a slow motion, Aurélien pushed his hand into his frock coat and undid the buttons on his trousers, slipping his hardening cock into the space between the layers. He shuddered at the touch of his own fingers against his erection. His hand moved slowly, spreading drops of precum along his length to ease the movement—had he not been within such a predicament, he'd gladly spit into his palm.

Defiling Father Celio with his perverse gaze was like oil on the fire, only serving to make the blaze burn even brighter. As he stroked himself, decaying any chance he may have of redemption in the eyes of the Lord, he watched the object of his affection look back. Unbreaking eye contact that only ended when the movement of Father Celio's tongue darted out to lick his lips like he tasted the most delicious feast.

Father Celio knew what humiliating things he did within The Church of Sanctuary. He knew and he watched. Father Celio *enjoyed* it. He liked watching. That was Aurélien's only wager, and as he stroked faster and faster—desperate for release, undeterred by those also within the service, he prayed. Not to God, of course, but to Father Celio himself. Prayed that it was not the fanciful, lust filled imagination that taunted him so, but the priest himself.

His prayers were answered most fruitfully as his climax came to him in a rush as powerful as a flood. Milky white seed coated his hand and, in that long moment of weakness, Aurélien brought his filthy fingers to his lips—licking away the evidence. His own seed was salty on his tongue and the immoral act only made his desire stronger. All the while, Father Celio's eyes were on him. Any chance he had succeeding in hiding his sinful ways was nil—boldly did he choose to use the opportunity to tempt the priest. An open invitation to be his.

Service dragged on and Aurélien, for once in his life, begged for the worship to be over. The only relief was the Eucharist. Father Celio pressed the body of Christ into the hand of his congregation. A chalice of wine was sipped from each patron most delicately, offered up by Deacon Wren—a younger man with wavy dark hair and pouty lips he couldn't deny thinking about more than once in the dead of night. If Father Celio had not consumed his world, the deacon would have captivated him with his dark brown eyes and long lashes until the end of time.

Aurélien knelt before the object of his worship and held out his hands.

Father Celio pressed a thumb to Aurélien's lip, willing him to open his mouth. He complied, savoring the pressure of the touch. He clasped behind his hands behind his back, obedient and poised to be made sinless again.

"Corpus Christi." He placed the body of Christ into his mouth, his fingers lingering upon his tongue. Father Celio was handed the chalice of wine by Deacon Wren, taking over the responsibility to offer the Blood of Christ to the final patron.

The silver chalice was pressed to Aurélien's lips with the withdrawal of the priest's hand. Slightly bitter red wine poured into his mouth, a small bit dribbling from the corner of his mouth. It ran down his throat, disappearing below the collar of his shirt. He swallowed, savoring every drop as it washed away the lingering taste of his own semen. Aurélien looked unto his mortal God and prayed—his most unholy prayers were answered with a divine hungry gaze meeting his.

Silence spread across The Church of Sanctuary, the only sound the clink of an empty silver chalice being placed onto a waiting tray held by Deacon Wren. All in attendance to the service had left whilst Aurélien lost himself in the bliss and sanctity that was being hand fed by his God. The three nuns who occupied the church's small convent stood behind him now, their gazes boring holes into his back leaving him feeling more exposed than he would have if he had stood before Father Celio as bare as the day he had been born.

Father Celio smiled, as handsome as even the most sought after courtesans, and offered to Aurélien his palms. "Take my hand. We will cleanse you, Lord Saint-Orlant. Make you anew in His image. You want that, do you not?"

Aurélien's eyes widened. He wanted that. Wanted to be perfect like Him. He placed his hands on Father Celio's, hot like an inferno against his own. "Save me, Father Celio, for I am sin itself."

Deacon Wren approached with a new tray, Aurélien only vaguely registering the world around him as the object of his obsession blessed him with his touch. The three nuns stepped closer, their footfalls the only sound in the church.

"And so, it shall be." Father Celio removed a dagger from the tray presented to him, the blade shining in the altar candles' light.

Aurélien swallowed, eyeing it warily as the priest pressed the tip of it to the center of his chest. He did not move and dared not fear the man before him. Father Celio would offer penance. Father Celio knew best.

"With this blade we cast out the false God and remake you in His image. May the true God be merciful. Dark Lord, save Your favored spawn from his prison!"

"Praise be to the Dark Lord!" Recited the clergy members as Father Celio pushed the silver dagger into his chest, tearing through flesh and meat. While he did so, he tore the family ring from Aurélien's finger.

Aurélien screamed as pain overcame his senses and every thread of his being was torn apart and rewoven by Father Celio's prayer. Blood rushed to escape his form, chased by the rapid beating of a frightened heart. He looked up at his mortal God and pleaded, grabbing at the handle of the dagger protruding from his chest.

Words would not escape his lips and he spoke them soundlessly, pleading for salvation while the world he saw turned to shades of darkness. An all-consuming darkness that came only with death.

†The Son's Awakening†

"Have we killed him?" Sister Isabel asked in a hush voice. "O' Dark Lord forgive us—we've killed him dead, sisters."

"A demon is not felled so easily, Sister Isabel," Father Celio remarked, placing a cold palm on Aurélien's forehead. Aurélien stirred, slowly blinking his eyes open at the touch—his sight hazy and out of focus.

"He's much more handsome now," Deacon Wren remarked.

"I think so too. Before it was like something was missing. Now I can see clearly, it was his horns!" Sister Myria observed, reaching to touch him but her hand was slapped away by Sister Isabel.

Sister Lavinia poured water into a bronze cup, pressing it to his lips. It was salvation to his dry mouth but did nothing for the swimming vision he possessed. Only slow blinking and patience cleared it.

The room slowly faded into his vision as his eyes adjusted to the low light. It was no room he had ever had the honor of being in, but still within the confines of The Church of Sanctuary, judging by the carved white stone arching above him—though the opulence of the front of the church had not spread to the modest bedroom he found himself residing in. Everything felt like a dream, and had it not been for the dull aching pain in his chest, he would have concluded it to be so.

He Who Bleeds

"What happened?" Aurélien croaked out, his voice hoarse—no doubt from his own screaming.

"You said his memories would merge," Deacon Wren said in an accusatory tone from his place leaned against the window beside the bed. Aurélien turned his attention to him and jolted at the sight of the other man. From dark tresses sprouted a pair of horns dusted with gold flakes, a slim tail of a similar shade tipped with a spade flicked about in annoyance like a mistreated feline.

"They should have. They *always* merge when I remove the ring," Father Celio stated. "He's been through something magnificent; his mind will catch up soon enough. Let's just hope *soon* is faster than his old master's whip."

"If we've created an invalid of His favorite son, the Dark Lord will be terribly furious," Sister Isabel bemoaned, disappointment in her voice.

Aurélien gawked as he fully saw everyone in the room with clear eyes finally. What surrounded him were not the kind clergy he knew, but demons. Demons surrounding the holy, godlike Father Celio.

"What *are* you?" Aurélien pressed, forcing himself to sit up despite the pain in his chest. He looked down briefly, finding his front bare save for layers of bandages wrapped around to keep his wound covered.

"He really is an invalid." Lavinia clicked her tongue. She too had changed, sporting horns from her auburn hair—skin cracked like old porcelain, a black swirling void filling the gaps. All of her teeth were sharp like fangs and he felt no shame in saying it made his skin crawl.

"*We* are what the humans call demons. Some call those like Wren and I incubi, but really, it's all the same unless you're someone exquisite," Celio explained, sitting himself on the edge of the bed, leaning in so close he could count the flecks of gold in his honey brown eyes. "And you are someone exquisite."

"You're all demons," he said in amazement. Aurélien looked upon the false priest before him in awe, drinking in his demonic visage. Clawed hands cupped his cheeks, and Aurélien, for once in his life, was not afraid of the emotions beginning to burst forth. Instead, he embraced them—pressing a hungry kiss to Celio's lips. It was returned with fervor, the incubus' hands slipping into his hair. The kiss lasted only a moment, but it was enough to steal away the panic that had been building inside.

"And you are the devil's scion, Little Love." Celio kissed him again, tasting the candied ginger Aurélien gifted Julius.

"The devil's... scion," Aurélien breathed out the words quietly.

"Mhm, and I have so kindly removed that foul curse you were under. Free of charge! Do forgive me for the methods I had to use, but Section 32, Clause F states the contract ends in death. You have died. For but a brief moment, darling, don't fret—and you're very much alive now, aren't you?" Celio sat up, a smile on his face.

"I died? I am a devil... and I died?" Aurélien's mind was reeling as he chipped away at the words. A small part of him wasn't surprised, like he always knew. There was no true reason he so easily believed the incubus before him, but it was like a piece finally fit into place. A soothing air swept over him, taking away his hesitation regarding everything before him.

"We stopped your heart," Wren said gruffly, far more focused on the state of his sharp claw-like nails than anything else.

"But only for a moment. Isabel brought you back like that," Myria said with a snap of her fingers for emphasis. The curly blonde hair that slipped from her veil bounced with the motion, distracting Aurélien almost enough to keep him from noticing the torn open gash ripping open her mouth, exposing part of her skull to the cool air of the church. It had long healed, scarred flesh reaching up towards her blue, almost milky white left eye. The eye's gaze bore into him, reminiscent of the black stallion his father kept. A watch eye, the stable hands had called it—and watch it did, sending a shiver down Aurélien's spine as it looked upon him.

"Yes, just a little zap!" Myria assured, wiggling corpse pale fingers before her that sparked with lightning arches between the slim digits. "It did more harm than the blade, can you believe that? No matter though, I brought you right back."

"Thank you," Aurélien choked out, though he didn't know what he was thanking them for. For sparing him? For freeing him? He wasn't even sure what exactly he had been freed of.

Compared to the other two sisters, Isabel looked rather normal, aside from her blood red skin. Aurélien feared what may linger beneath her habit. As if to answer his question, she shook her hands excitedly, her sleeves slipping down to expose a speckling of black and silver scales along her forearms, contrasting beautifully against her flesh.

"You're most welcome, Lord Saint-Orlant," Myria said, curtsying to him like he was some dignified prince.

Suddenly it occurred to him, if he was a devilspawn— what possible repulsions did he possess now. Had he too sprung wings and horns like his beloved Celio and Wren? He wished to rush to the nearest mirror and peer for hours. He needed to know how uprooted his life truly was. And if he was truly the devil's scion, was he Lucifer's young? That beautiful fallen angel he so admired from the Bible. Was he truly His?

"Everyone, leave us. Our Dark Prince needs his rest. This will have taken its toll on him," Celio instructed.

The demons in the room hesitated, the once God-fearing sisters looking between one another before scurrying from the room.

"If I hear moaning, I'm burning this church to the fucking ground," Wren warned, pushing himself off of the wall.

Celio laughed as the door slammed closed behind Wren. "Don't mind him. He's jealous."

"Jealous? Why would he be jealous?" Aurélien's mind was still reeling from everything he had been told thus far.

"Of course he is, Little Love, he doesn't have you like I do. He's upset I claimed you before he could. He was the first to begin our mission, but I found you before anyone else. Stumbling into my fraud of a church like a lost soul." Celio pushed him back down onto the bed, straddling him. Aurélien's heart beat louder than a locomotive, blood roaring in his ears as it made its way directly to his cock. "I do have you, don't I?"

"You… and me?" Aurélien said, as eloquent as a drunk.

"I saw what you did during my sermon. Naughty. Were you thinking about me? Ah, don't answer that—I know you were. I've been dreaming about our last night together all day, too. It isn't often I get so properly bred with so much carnage around me. You were like an animal." Celio pressed his lips to Aurélien's, stealing his breath away once again.

Aurélien's hands landed hesitantly on the small of the incubus' waist, the fabric course under his fingers. He kissed with every ounce of desire he possessed for the man, afraid that when he next opened his eyes he'd find himself at the center of an elaborate jest.

"That's it, darling, give yourself to me. Body and soul," Celio purred.

Aurélien wanted nothing more than to do so. To be his forevermore but, regrettably, he had questions. Ones only Celio would be able to answer. "I want nothing more, Fa—Celio. I have questions, first."

"Go ahead. Ask your questions. I'm sure you have plenty."

"Who exactly is my father?"

"He has many names you may know. Lucifer. The Morning Star. The first fallen angel. You are His lone spawn on this plane at present—He doesn't create life from Himself unless He sees potential, nor does He if the contract presented is subpar. You are so powerful and perfect, yet you don't know your full glory. That damned contract kept you oh so restrained," Celio explained. He sat back, no longer as fixated on urging Aurélien on.

"What were the terms of my contract? Are we sure it's broken?"

Celio shrugged. The silver and onyx pectoral cross he wore swayed and, for the first time, Aurélien saw how mutilated the piece was—torn apart by a beast with claws. "I know some of the terms, naturally, I was—am your assistant. A double agent, if you will. Around the time you came into your dark inheritance, Wren and myself began our search for the lost spawn. Our job was simple: keep you safe and guide you through your dark desires. Imagine our surprise when we found you a God-fearing mortal still chained by some invisible mortal master. The Dark Lord instructed us to corrupt a church and guide you until we found the owner of your leash."

Dorian Valentine

Aurélien listened with rapt attention as Celio continued on.

"While we never found the owner, we did learn quite a bit. With a generous blessing from the Dark Lord, your master was convinced to begin sending his requests directly to me. You were being instructed to kill on your master's behalf. Mostly aristocrats and politicians. Those who offended your master in some way. I, being such a kind lover, assisted—all the while reporting back to both your master and the Dark Lord."

"Can my father—the Dark Lord, could He not simply tell me who my master is?" Aurélien asked, brows furrowed as he pieced through everything.

"If only it were so simple." The false priest sighed, a pout forming on his lips. "No, He is bound as much by a contract as you were. What He can say is you were born from a contract of His own. Your birth was beneficial to both sides.

"And my memories? I take it I am missing some part of myself." Aurélien raised his hands before himself for the first time, bewildered by the pallid corpse-like tone of his flesh and the claws he now bore. "What do I look like?"

"As handsome as the day I married you," Celio teased, lacing his own clawed fingers with his. Aurélien's heartbeat quickened at those words, even if he knew deep down they couldn't possibly be true. "Handsome. Beautiful. If you were an incubus, I fear the rest of us would starve. Let's see… your ears for one are different. Pointed like the fae, Little Love. As pretty as one too."

Aurélien unlaced his hand from Celio's and reached up to feel, tracing the long-pointed cartilage that replaced the rounded ears he was familiar with.

Celio continued on as he used a finger to trace one of the horns sprouting from his hairline. "Your horns are so adorable. Small, only because you never keep them long enough to grow to full size. Next are your eyes. They were dark before, but now they're the red of the hottest of coals. Burning embers of Hellfire—not many would notice, but I do. They're captivating."

A shiver ran through Aurélien as a finger twirled around and around the small horns sprouting from his head. It was pleasure coursing through his veins, everything the incubus did set his skin on fire with desire. "What else?"

"Give me time to recite my poetry, Little Love, it's not every day I get to wax on and on like this." The incubus kissed him again, slow, and mellow like one might savor a glass of champagne. "You still have your pretty dark hair—it still curls so perfectly around your ears here."

Another kiss. The incubus sampled him. Like Aurélien's lips were an appetizer to keep him fed as he awaited a long-anticipated meal. Aurélien's hands touched, only faintly at first— so afraid his hands would burn upon the unholy man.

"Take my body, darling. Take it and you shall remember if we are so lucky. We have lost many hours with each other, if I cannot bring you to remembrance as easily as I do orgasm, then I'm afraid you may be in for a long forgetful time."

Aurélien needed no other urging. Years of yearning were coming to an end, and he would be damned by the false God if he let something as unimportant as a new tail deter him from taking what was his. He crushed their lips together again, hands tearing at the false vestments upon the man.

His tail—something he would stare at for hours when given a moment alone, flicked about behind him in excitement as he pressed the incubus down onto the small, rickety bed they occupied.

Laughter lingered between their kisses, amusement falling off of Celio in waves that he seemed unable—or unwilling—to contain. Aurélien didn't care if they shared laughter between their kisses, there was a humor in how his tail flicked about and knocked over forgotten medical supplies. Little glass vials fell to the floor, clattering, but did not break. Lips fell to Celio's neck as his collar was torn away, his clothing shreds before their eyes.

"What an excitable mate," Celio said, with no lack of amusement in his tone. He spread his legs further for Aurélien, welcoming and accepting him in full. "Are you planning on breeding me? Like a dog in heat?"

Aurélien snapped his head up, wide eyed. "What? I can do that?"

Celio tilted his head back as he roared with laughter, giggling like he was told the most humorous joke. "No, Little Love, oh how regrettably you cannot. But we have had the most wondrous time trying together, haven't we? Well… I suppose you don't remember."

The devilspawn's heart fluttered in his chest. "Help me remember."

It wasn't a request. It was a demand. One Aurélien was positive the incubus beneath him would agree to rapidly.

A smug smile spread across Celio's flushed face. He slipped fingers into Aurélien's dark hair, guiding him back down into his warm embrace. Skilled fingers undid the buttons on Aurélien's trousers, pushing them down without even breaking the kiss.

He Who Bleeds

His hand wrapped around Aurélien's hard cock, stroking slowly—smearing precum across his length. It was dry but Aurélien found he didn't care at the moment. Just the simplest touch from Celio was like a fantasy—something far more intimate than a dream or passing thought. This was everything he had wanted and more. To have the false priest beneath him making soft, pleased sounds against his lips had him accepting how quickly he would cum before they were even fully undressed.

"Is it true?" Aurélien asked, breaking their kiss so he could further undress the incubus beneath him. With each inch of flesh exposed to the chilled air of the church, he laid a kiss.

"Is what true, Little Love?" Celio asked, resting a hand in his hair again, pushing his head further down.

"That you incubi feed on sex."

"You have such a way with words! What an ability you have—to simplify it so." Celio laughed, raising his hips as Aurélien removed his trousers. "We feed on lust and desire—and the occasional mortal flesh."

Aurélien swallowed, his mind now filled with the sight of Celio's nude form. His cock was hard, leaking against his lower stomach with a flush across his supple flesh. He looked as though he had already been fucked properly, lips wet with their shared spit.

"Mh—you like the view, don't you? I can taste your desire. So sweet, like sugar." Celio wrapped a hand around his own cock and stroked slowly, keeping his eyes locked with Aurélien's. "I can feel what my target feels. Every touch, every emotion. I know you want me."

Aurélien's mouth went dry, watching the sinful movement of his hand—transfixed by the strokes, eyes trained on the milky white pearl beading from the tip of his cock. He wondered what it tasted like. Would it be as sweet as his lips? "I do. For years I have sinned with you in my thoughts. You have enthralled me from the moment I cast eyes upon you."

Celio huffed a laugh, hooking a leg around Aurélien to bring him in closer, the devilspawn slipping in between his legs like a missing puzzle piece. Aurélien's cock rubbed against Celio's, and a delighted whimper left the incubus' lips. With a slight curl to his lip Celio said, "That's cute and all, but I need you to fuck me right now, not make love to me."

"Oil?" he asked, eloquently, looking around the room for some sort of lubrication.

"No need. I *love* it rough. Now pin me to the bed and fuck me like a good little demon." Celio released him from his grip, shuffling himself so he was sitting again.

Aurélien watched for a moment, calculating his options, and found there was only one satisfactory response to being commanded by one so undoubtedly beneath him, even if the demands made his cock throb in excitement. He pushed it aside and, with less effort than he expected, dragged Celio by a horn to his feet. The far wall, one void of any windows and few adornments, was perfect for his intended course of action.

As he forced Celio's chest against the wall, Aurélien grabbed a vial from the bedside. He caged Celio in against the wall with his larger body, mouthing against his neck to leave his marks. They would show above the vestments, and all would know of the broken vow of this seductive priest. The church patrons will see him and smell the claiming scents Aurélien leaves. Celio was his to take, willingly given by the incubus. There was nothing more exciting than to have such a fine specimen in his arms.

He Who Bleeds

Uncapping the vial filled their small space with the medicinal scent of various herbs and Aurélien let the oil drip onto the cleft of Celio's rear. The incubus quivered as chilled liquid ran down his skin and Aurélien couldn't help but be fascinated. He had been with other men in his time—hushed meetings during University and lustful meetings with Julius within The Orchid House, but this was something entirely different. His thoughts were not his own, but the desires of someone lurking deep within him. The demon within wished to torture this priest with pleasure.

Aurélien coated his fingers with oil and knelt behind Celio in worship, his right hand against his waist to keep him pinned in place. Had he truly wished to leave, Aurélien was positive he would wriggle his way out, but Celio remained and Aurélien continued. He had a long list of desires to go through and the night was only so long.

"Stay against the wall," Aurélien instructed. "I mean to make art of you."

"Oh, I do adore your art, Little Love. What have you planned for tonight? Flaying? Clamps? Don't keep me guessing, I'll be good if you tell me." Celio wriggled with excitement.

Celio's rear was plump in his hands, and he had no problem spreading him to view his prize. Aurélien wasted no time, pressing the flat of his tongue against his hole. The hitch in Celio's breath only motivated him. It was music to his ears, and he would compose something beautiful with his new instrument. He licked several times, until Celio was pliant above him and relaxed.

"Mh—you don't do this too often," Celio remarked, as pleased as a cat who caught the caged songbird, while pressing back for more. "Why don't you put that fat cock of yours inside already?"

"No. I am creating art. Music. I wish to hear it." Aurélien licked again. He wanted to taste all of him, every inch of delicious flesh—all for him to devour. The whines and choked off moans fed him as if he was the incubus in the room. Between his thighs, his cock stood proudly, blushed and aching from neglect.

Aurélien pressed the tip of his tongue inside, thrusting it in and out, saliva flowing freely as he spread it deep within. Under his hands, Celio quivered—his body betraying the cocky tone he carried. He spent several blissful minutes tasting his incubus until his hole was pliant against his tongue. The devilspawn pulled back, examined his work, then spit. A muffled moan came from above. Such a beautiful sound, better than any orchestra he had chanced upon.

"Why are you torturing me?" Celio whined, turning slightly to show Aurélien the pout on his lips.

It did little to speed up Aurélien's actions. He would be slow and methodical with his work. Art took time. Composing a symphony could not occur in moments. It took a skilled creator. It took patience, above all. The reward would be worth the agony of waiting. Aurélien pushed an oil coated finger into Celio's spit slick hole. "Not torture."

"Ah—you bastard. Quit teasing me!" Celio's tail flicked about in annoyance until Aurélien grabbed it and placed a kiss upon the base.

"You live for my cock, don't you?" Aurélien asked, moving his finger slowly. He watched, transfixed—he needed him, wanted to claim him. But not yet. In time. For now, he would savor the experience.

"I will perish without it," Celio confided, pressing back to demand more.

Aurélien, just this once, conceded. He pressed three fingers into his willing hole. "You will not starve. I fed you earlier."

Celio let his shoulders drop, holding onto the wall for purchase, pathetic moans falling from his lips. Aurélien mouthed the plush meat of his ass while he fucked his fingers into him, biting and marking every inch he saw. He wanted the false priest to remember this moment each time he sat down. They would mark the sins committed within the unholy church.

"Good boy. I will claim you wholly and you will remember who you belong to." Aurélien curled his fingers, pressing against the incubus' prostate. "Would you like that?"

"Nhn! Y-Yes, yes please! Please, my prince. Please—please claim me. Grant me release. Show me your favor. I beg of you!" Celio gasped out his pleas, choked out moans punctuating his words. It was delicious, nearly enough to crack his resolve.

Aurélien stood, pressing Celio against the wall still. His prey's tail wrapped around his thigh, bringing him even closer. With a hand loosely around the incubus' throat, he forced his back to arch—the curve of the false priest's body was a thing of beauty, one Aurélien wished to see carved into marble. He kept his fingers moving, stretching him open until wet, sloppy sounds filled the space between them. "Your voice is so beautiful when you plead for mercy. You're singing a hymn for me."

"They have ah—ah—always been for you!"

Finally, Aurélien was satisfied, tilting the other's head so he could kiss him deeply. His tongue slipped into Celio's mouth, and the demon sucked, pleased hums slipping from their lips.

As he pulled his fingers out, leaving the incubus whining even more, Celio said, "Don't use any more oil. I want to feel the stretch."

"It'll hurt." Aurélien stroked his cock slowly, spreading the beads of precum from his tip down the shaft. He smacked his throbbing length against Celio's hole. Vague memories surfaced, barely there thoughts regarding their time together. The clearest memory was drenched in blood and gore—one he'd give anything to experience firsthand. He knew how blissful fucking the false priest would be and he had to tamper his excitement to keep from rutting into him like a beast. A part of Aurélien was afraid of the shift he felt overtaking himself, rewriting everything he knew but at the moment, his mind was elsewhere. Two minds melding could be ignored in favor of pleasuring a demon of pleasure.

"I want it to hurt. When it's you, even pain is pleasure," Celio informed, choking out around the pressure against his throat. Aurélien pressed fingers into his always running mouth to silence him, a pink tongue licking them clean of their collective filth.

"Do you take sick pleasure in being a demon in holy clothes?"

Celio nodded his head, gasping as Aurélien pushed his cock into him. He reached back, grasping for his lover, claws cutting into Aurélien's flesh with his desperation.

"Say it, my love—I want to hear it." Aurélien pulled back, watching the place they met. Celio was sinfully tight and the gasping moans leaving the incubus' lips tested his resolve. He snapped his hips forward, drinking in the loud whine from the false priest.

"I *love* it. Those stupid—ah fucks don't know every prayer is one to you, my p-prince. Oh! Yes! Again, again please—o' merciful Dark Prince, again. Break me—breed me. Claim me!"

His resolve was cracked, Aurélien lost control as he listened to such sweet praise that sounded like a prayer. He fucked into Celio like he hated him, the only sound in the room the sound of the skin against skin and desperate moaning.

Aurélien kept them against the wall, the rough stone cutting into Celio's skin—the faint scent of blood only spurring on Aurélien's desire. He had a desire to taste it. As his orgasm crept up on him, Aurélien gave into the curiosity. He bit into the meat of Celio's shoulder, fangs sinking into the flesh without resistance.

Celio gasped out part of his name, cumming with his neglected, untouched cock. Aurélien came inside of him while he tasted the sweetness of his blood. He withdrew his fangs, licking over the wound as they both came down from their orgasmic high.

"Biting mh—you don't do that often. How does my flesh taste?" Celio asked between heavy breaths.

Aurélien pulled out and reached down to remove Celio's tail from his thigh. He picked up the false priest and brought him to the small bed to rest. Celio wrapped himself in the warm blankets and Aurélien abandoned his search for something to clean their mess, picking up a clean rag from the tray of medical supplies. Celio lazily sat up again, yanked the rag from Aurélien's hand and began to clean himself up.

"I'm a new man. Not only the demon you knew, but the human as well. I am both, yet neither," Aurélien concluded, kissing his forehead. He grabbed the rag and took over cleaning the cum from inside of Celio, ignoring his pouts.

"And I am very excited to get to know him."

†Normalcy†

Julius became a fixture within Aurélien's townhouse—as Father Beausoliel visiting the premises day in and day out would raise the brow of even the most atheist person in society. Though The Church of Sanctuary was a relatively small place of admittedly false worship with an even smaller cloister, Father Celio was a known figure amongst the public. The gossip would spread, and with so many flooding the streets of London for the season, Aurélien's once quiet oasis would spark the most delicious rumor of the year before spring even officially turned to summer.

Over the course of several weeks, Aurélien had come into his own once again. Though some aspects of his mind remained fractured, with each passing day he felt less and less like two beings occupying the same vessel. For days, he had been bedridden with splitting migraines and shifting forms that left him nearly to the brink of sobbing in agony. Celio was by his side through it all, providing relief through incubus spit and the gentlest of touches.

With time, and between long claiming sessions that Celio insisted were good for his health, Aurélien came into his power. Some were easy to manage—the slipping between forms, the flick of Hellfire between fingers, the exciting ability of flight that took them both high above the London smog, and according to Celio, the very important ability to retract his claws. Though Aurélien was learning rather quickly to not trust the guidance of the incubus wholeheartedly. The man only had one thing on his mind, and while Aurélien was thrilled to comply with those demands, he could not spend his entire life in bed feeding his incubus.

April 27th, 1874, began like any other, aside from the anticipation of his sister's arrival—alerted via a telegram's delivery during the early afternoon the day before. Breakfast was followed by feeding an increasingly pleased incubus.

The season was well underway when Theia finally arrived to spend several weeks within his townhouse, ruining the pleasant afternoon he was having with Celio. She called it being fashionably late while he called it being a bother and a nuisance. Despite this, he did care for his sister and allowed her into his townhouse with open arms. Theia looked more like her mother than their shared father, soft blonde hair, and a delicately round face. The journey from their family estate, located northwest of Birmingham in the town of Wolverhampton, had left her tired around the eyes.

"Are you ill?" she asked, in lieu of a proper greeting. Her blue eyes, which seemed even brighter when compared to the navy color of her lace accented promenading gown, scrutinized him. Her lady's maid scurried past with two of Theia's smaller bags in hand, stopping only to offer a haphazard curtsy before bustling through to her rooms.

"Ill? Why would you think that?" Aurélien asked, twisting the sealing ring Celio had given him around his finger to sooth his nerves. He would know if his true form slipped out, if only by the angry flicking of his tail when it found itself wrongfully detained within his trousers. Still, he thanked the ring for its assistance in keeping his demonic form at bay.

"You look tired. Around the eyes. Not sleeping well?" Theia asked, coming up close to study her older brother's face.

"I'm sleeping fine," Aurélien assured, "I trust your journey here was without trouble?"

"It was uneventful. Margaret kept me company, as always."

Celio swept into the room disguised as Julius, dressed in what was clearly Aurélien's house robe, the hem dragging on the floor as he walked. "I can hardly believe that—oh! You have a visitor."

"Who is this?" Theia asked, her brow raising as she studied the man before her.

Aurélien glanced at the smaller man who came to stand by his side. "As I said when you came to spend the season with me, my sister would also be staying. Theia, may I introduce to you my good friend, Julius Beausoliel. Julius, this is Lady Theia Saint-Orlant."

Theia held a gloved hand out to Julius, the incubus taking it delicately and placing a featherlight kiss to her hand. "Charmed, I'm sure."

"It is I who is charmed, Lady Saint-Orlant. Such beautiful women rarely cross my path. I must thank fate for bringing our worlds together, if only for this short time."

The young woman blushed, bringing her free hand to her cheek to hide the flush. "Your wife is a very lucky woman, Mr. Beausoliel."

"I have no wife. I'm afraid I have a life as a confirmed bachelor ahead of me. It's why I've come to spend the season here in Knightsbridge." Celio smiled—a charming smile no doubt laced with his sensual magic to promptly win over Theia. "Unlike my brother who has taken a vow of celibacy with the church, I have my own lack of status to blame for the issue."

He Who Bleeds

Celio guided them through the townhouse as if he owned it, taking them into the library where light tea and cakes were served before the fire to welcome in the afternoon properly. Conversation was kept friendly—tales of their time apart and quips from Celio to fill in the silence.

Theia placed her empty teacup upon the table, folding her hands upon her lap most seriously. "There is something I wish to discuss, Aurélien. Alone, if possible. My apologies, Mr. Beausoliel. It's a family matter, I'm sure you understand."

"No offense taken. I shall take my leave. It was a pleasure to meet you, Lady Saint-Orlant." Celio stood and left without much fuss, which surprised Aurélien more than anything.

Once the doors to the library closed, Theia's expression turned solemn. She poured herself a cup of tea, a silence washing over the sunset filled room.

"What did you need to discuss?" Aurélien asked, though he was not overly concerned. Despite living a great distance from family, should someone have taken ill, he would have received a telegram—or simply a letter, had the individual been of a distant relation.

"I have an ulterior motive for coming, aside from looking for my own marriage prospects. Father is growing concerned. You are nearly thirty-one now without even a prospective fiancée," Theia began, pausing to stir a sugar cube into her tea. "Father has a proposition in mind, if you will."

"I have a feeling I know where this is going."

"I'm sure you do. Father has given you until the end of the season to find a prospective bride."

Aurélien sighed. "And if I fail this tiresome task?"

"You will have two options. Either give up your inheritance and any claim to the family name or marry someone he has selected." Theia smiled wryly. This was no doubt as unpleasant a task for her as it was for Aurélien to receive.

"Father is as demanding as always. Do you know who he has in mind? Surely some political arrangement that will bring in ties he's been chasing for aeons."

"Miss Lucille Bradshaw. Her family is in the steel mill business, from my understanding. She has no siblings, so her husband is set to inherit."

"As expected, Father is nothing if not calculating."

"He is. It is what keeps us safe." A small silence passed between them before Theia spoke again. "Your Mr. Beausoliel is an interesting gentleman. Where on Earth did you meet him?"

Lying, while typically a demon's talent, did not come naturally to Aurélien. He found himself absolutely horrendous if not given adequate time to spin a tale. He much preferred telling the raw truth and watching the person squirm while trying to decide if he spoke the truth or was toying with their mind. Sometimes it was both. Oftentimes it was both. Regardless, he was already keeping secrets from her—the small tedious detail that they shared no actual blood in their veins—but now he must hide the true nature of his relationship with Celio. At the very least, Celio had laid the foundation for a perfectly believable lie one he could spin with hopeful ease. "His brother is Father Celio Beausoliel, a priest within The Church of Sanctuary. I frequent the church, as you know. We met a few years ago during Mass and became fast friends over a drink afterwards."

"I can't picture him as a God-fearing man."

"Julius fears little and God is not among their numbers."

†Answers†

The demons who resided within the false church, as well as Aurélien, were undoubtedly confused as the days ticked by and not a single mention of the contract being terminated came about. Truthfully, Aurélien didn't know what exactly they were looking for. Was his true father supposed to reach up and claim him in flames of Hellfire and smoke? Was there supposed to be an army marching?

An answer came mere days after Theia's arrival at his townhouse. It wasn't as glamourous as a personal visit from dear old father Lucifer, but one from his old master. Celio had been lounging within Aurélien's bed late one night, a book held open on his bare thigh as he curled close to the devilspawn.

Celio gasped like all the air had been sucked from his lungs, his various glamours falling away to reveal his demon form. With his eyes rolled back, he clutched at this throat, a voice unlike his own ripped itself from his throat.

"Next target. Earl Jonathan Brighton. Files with the demon Wren. Soon. Be a good pet."

Aurélien watched in horror, his hands shaking as he tried to settle the writhing incubus upon his bed. He pressed his hands upon his body, pulling him close and attempted to cease his shaking and trembling lover as the hold the voice had over him faded. "Celio? Are you with me?"

It took several moments of deep breathing for Celio to regain his ability to speak. Celio rubbed a hand over his forehead. "I'm okay. Been over a decade and these things still get the best of me."

"Was that my... father?" Aurélien asked with a furrow to his brows.

"No, the Dark Lord sends His regards in much more glamourous ways. Suicidal confessionals are a favorite of His," Celio sat up, drawing the blankets close. Aurélien couldn't blame him, he imagined such an experience was remarkably violating. To lose control of one's body was something he was deeply familiar with. "This was your cheeky little owner. The bastard seems totally unaware of the broken contract."

"Are we entirely sure it has been broken?"

Celio shrugged then used a finger to loop a stray piece of hair behind his ear. "I don't know, Little Love, I think it has been."

"You don't *know*. You stabbed me through the heart, and you don't know? Celio, my love, you could have killed me with the stunt you pulled." Aurélien didn't mean to scold. He was grateful he finally knew himself for the first time in his life. It was a blessing to be whole, one he planned to be eternally grateful to Celio for, yet he couldn't help but be enraged.

"I'm an incubus, Little Love. I don't deal in contracts and fine details." He pouted. "Everything led us all to believe stopping the heart long enough to make you dead by the laws of Hell would be enough to break the contract. We can assume something worked, you're whole again after all."

"*Nearly* whole," Aurélien corrected, pinching the bridge of his nose between his fingers. "This is potentially an issue. I will need to assassinate this Earl Brighton. If my contract hasn't been voided properly, I will be punished as per Section 3, Clause B."

"You know I'll help you like the good little assistant I am, darling. We'll take him out real quick, he's probably some old fuck anyways."

Aurélien was quiet for a moment, thinking through an assortment of futures that could lay before them. If the contact is only partially broken, which as it stood was certainly the case, he could trace it back to his owner. He could finally know once and for all who stole away his life. The master who desecrated his being with clause upon clause of chaining words that kept him captive like a pet could finally be unmasked. "You've never spoken to my owner in person, correct?"

"Right. I use a set of mirror books to give him the details. What I write down is instantly copied into the one he owns."

"And are we certain that my owner is a man?"

Celio nodded, curling up against Aurélien's side again. "Yes. The Dark Lord was able to give us at least that amount of information regarding the contract holder."

"So, what we know is this: The Dark Lord was offered a deal—the creation of a spawn in exchange for the spawn's services until death."

"That's the contract boiled down to the essentials," the incubus confirmed.

"Why would my father need a contract to create me?"

"Hm… now that's a question, isn't it? Demons—incubi and succubi aside—can only reproduce when contracted to. Keeps our population culled. If every demon who wanted a hoard of spawn got a hoard of spawn, there'd be no more humans. This rule pertains to His Highness as well." Celio explained it patiently, all the while occupying his hands with Aurélien's fingers.

"And incubi—why are they exempt?"

"Half-human, half-demon. They're called cambions. Like dhampirs, they're strong and useful to the full blooded. Good padding for armies and good at creating mischief within the mortal realm." Celio shrugged again. "Us incubi, and succubi, mind you, are born from Lilith and her witches. Our offspring are less than, much the same as we lilithspawn are."

"I'm not one of these cambions then? I am the creation of the Dark Lord and a human woman, presumably."

"No. You may have been incubated within a human woman, but you are wholly from the Dark Lord's seed."

"Would the human woman have been willing?"

"Possibly. There's no real telling. Her husband could have sold her womb. She could have just been unlucky. Or perhaps she's the real contract holder. I couldn't possibly say for certain, Little Love." Celio paused to crack the knuckles on Aurélien's left ring finger, popping filling the silence before he continued. "Why all the questions?"

"I need my facts straight to decide my course of action. There's much I don't know."

A comfortable silence hung between them while Aurélien thought over the information he possessed. The quiet was only broken by Celio's inability to keep quiet or still. "What are you thinking in that handsome mind of yours, hm?"

"Does the birth of a spawn kill the mother?"

"With cambions, no. They're not any more difficult than a human spawn. The chances of death are the same. A devilspawn though… there's very few of them. Every millennium one is born if the Dark Lord is so lucky. They say that the spawn claws its way out of the host womb. She'd die before that; the pain is more than a human can handle." Celio explained everything carefully, so full of patience. If someone had been asking Aurélien such tedious, elementary questions, he was sure he'd be annoyed before the third ever left their mouth.

"Why, pray tell, does an immortal like the Dark Lord want a child?"

Celio puckered his lips and awaited his demands to be fulfilled before any more answers were given—a hungry kiss that left both gasping and wanting more. "The Dark Lord has several children, the oldest came shortly after His great fall from the Heavens. They are His most loyal generals, after those who fell alongside Him, of course. The spawn are more demon than most, a perfect soldier for His growing armies. Waiting a few decades for a general is hardly an issue for someone as magnificent as He."

"Thank you, Celio. You're always a wonderful pest on my shoulder." Aurélien was satisfied with his line of questioning, for now. He already knew there'd be dozens more to ask, but it was late. Celio was just as, if not more, tired than he was. There was one thing he learned from all of this. His owner was someone he knew. Someone he trusted. The instant he thought about it for more than a moment, it all became clear. The secrecy, the hiding—all of it. He had lived with his mind split for over twelve years because of one man afraid of having the truth become known. As he listened to Celio's explanation, only one name came to him again and again. Baron Montague Edwin Saint-Orlant—his human father. The pieces fell into place so quickly, so easily, that there was no other option in his mind. Baron Montague Edwin Saint-Orlant had condemned him. For that he had to die.

"I can hear your thoughts turning," Celio accused, tilting his head back to look up at the devilspawn—his horns poking Aurélien's chest enough to hurt. His pout said, very clearly: *give me attention.*

"Mm. I believe I know who my owner is—it is an unsettling conclusion."

"Don't leave me in suspense, darling." Celio listened with full attention, sitting up to look at him so quickly he nearly knocked his head into Aurélien's chin.

"A little suspense is fun, don't you think?" Aurélien sighed. "I think, no—I know who it is. Sloppy. Disgusting man. He wanted my mind split so I wouldn't connect the pieces with such ease. It's that damned man. Baron Montague Edwin Saint-Orlant, my human 'father'. I know he's a scheming bastard, but this? Bargaining with the devil for social gains? It really shouldn't surprise me, but it does."

"Do you know what separates a human from a demon?" Celio asked, his tail wrapping around Aurélien's. It felt like a warm hug, familiar and safe.

"Aside from the obvious lineage? No, can't say I do."

"Demons have the inability to feel love. We feel..." He paused to grasp the right words. "We feel what we think is love. But it will never be the same love a human feels. Other than that, humans are just as selfish and rotten as they make us demons out to be."

Aurélien paused at this. He thought of everyone he considered close and sure enough, while he cared for each to some degree, he would not say love was the word he'd use. He tolerated Theia, he missed the concept of a mother, he loathed his father—and, most importantly, he adored Celio. Lusted for him. Craved him. But love? The thought hardly crossed his mind. He had certainly said it, but had he ever truly meant it?

"What I mean is this: that human is as terrible as the rest of us, probably even worse, and if he didn't feel love, I'd call him a demon too." Celio pressed a kiss to the base of each of Aurélien's horns. "Be angry with him. Be furious. We will *destroy* him in the Dark Lord's name. No, in your name, Little Love, in your unholy name. He will be the first blood offering for the magnificent General Au—the Dark Lord's most anticipated scion. And, when his blood flows free, we shall dance in it. We will fuck in it. His soul will writhe in agony as we soil it with our victory."

"What glorious plans you create with that beautiful mind of yours, darling."

"Your praise is like a drug." Celio grinned, reaching over to snuff out the lights, bathing the entire room in nothing but the warm glow of the fire and the thin moonbeams that cut through the clouds of London. He curled up close to Aurélien, lazily kissing his worries away.

Aurélien smiled. Despite everything he learned, things that should be making his head spin with worry and uncharted anxiety, he felt nothing but calmness when beside Celio. "I will gladly fuel your addiction."

†Godless Hedonism†

Earl Jonathan Brighton was younger than his typical targets. Usually those on the unfavorable end of his blade were older gentlemen who long since vacated the classification of young. Aurélien had, in fact, been quite good friends with his target during university and still, on occasion, joined the slightly older gentleman at one of the various clubs located off of St. James Street. During university they had occasionally entangled with one another late at night, fucking out regressed urges in the hopes of discarding them in time to find a good wife upon graduation.

At the age of thirty-four, much like Aurélien, Brighton had not married, but there were rumors of quite loud women in the East End claiming his parentage of the odd child here or there. This was an easy explanation for the hit on his life, but Aurélien knew the truth. It was a statement from his so-called father. Montague knew. He knew what Celio had done to Aurélien, and he was *laughing*. Thus, Aurélien was tasked with murdering one of his few mortal friends.

The task was a clear test. Kill Brighton and the theory that Aurélien had regained partial control of his life may cease being scrutinized. If he refused, well—there's no telling what kind of carnage such a thing would bring about. The ease in which Aurélien made the choice only solidified in his own mind that what Celio told him was positively true. He was the devil's scion, and he most certainly could not feel love.

He Who Bleeds

Upon learning of his plan to host a soirée, Theia promptly took the helm. She called his methods sloppy and stole away his registry of vendors along with his list of guests. Aurélien let her and only emphasized the importance of inviting one Earl Jonathan Brighton. She seemed to have it in her mind that this was a kind attempt by him to assist in her quest to find a proper husband. After all, who would be more perfect than an older, well-established man like Brighton? Had this been any other occasion, Aurélien would agree with her—Brighton would have been an excellent match. Unfortunately for her, and even more so for him, Brighton would not live through the night.

Theia was a wonder on such short notice, and by the end of the following week, a crowd of close friends and those she wished to gain acquaintanceship with were gathered within his townhouse. Aurélien's home was typically spacious for himself and the handful of staff in his employ, but now, with dozens of people milling about, it seemed as small as a pauper's room.

"Your sister has planned an extravagant gathering, Little Love," Celio commented, offering Aurélien a glass of wine. He sipped from his own, giving Aurélien plenty of time to admire his appearance. For this soirée he had shed his Julius glamour, instead appearing as his Father Celio—a recently retired clergy member. He wore a garment of silk and brocade in deep red hues. Upon his fingers were golden rings, all borrowed from Aurélien's collection. Celio's ink black hair hung loose, slightly wavy from the braid he had worn for most of the day. Beautiful like the rising sun. Aurélien wished to whisk him away, far from the undeserving gaze of the humans making merry within his townhouse. He wanted to keep Celio hidden away, kept. Safe. Wholly his.

"Just for tonight use my name. Those of our persuasion are still destined for the jailhouse—and my lock picking skills are not as refined as I'd like."

"Aurélien," Celio purred, batting his eyelashes at him. "I will be on my best behavior until told otherwise."

"That's what terrifies me, Father Celio, your best behavior is that of a tramp," Aurélien teased before knocking back the last dregs of wine.

Celio smirked, putting a hand on his slim waist. Aurélien's eyes followed the movement. "I much prefer *daddy* to Father."

"With the way you moan on my cock? I can't imagine you earning that title," he remarked, voice low so those milling about close by couldn't hear such a promiscuous phrase coming from their host's mouth.

A laugh came from the incubus' lips, the man smiling wide. Everything seemed to please him, everything was exciting and each thing he did was for his own entertainment before anything else. "Where's our target?"

"Nine o'clock. By the mantle, admiring the portrait there." Aurélien pointed with his chin to a tall blond man with a well-trimmed beard. Brighton stood with a glass of brandy in hand, head tilted up to admire the artwork above. At his side was Theia, hands clasped before her as she spoke to him. It was rather pathetic to watch her bumble about trying to catch his eye, ignored in favor of oil on canvas in Aurélien's likeness.

"He's pretty," Celio commented, a sourness in his voice.

"Do I detect a hint of jealousy, darling?"

"Au contraire, Little Love. I know I have nothing to worry about. You are mine. Anyone who challenges my claim will die."

He Who Bleeds

Aurélien chuckled and walked his way towards their new target. Their admittedly messy past of dormitory room romps late in the night were enough to give him the slightest pause when it came to assassinating him but, when it came down to it, it was either Brighton or himself—and Aurélien cared for himself more than some human. "Brighton! It has been some time. I see you've met my sister."

Brighton turned and smiled. "Saint-Orlant, it has been ages. How have you been? We've missed you down at the club. Come by for a drink some time or have you finally taken the leap into the clergy?"

Theia covered her mouth with a gloved hand, giggling. "Oh, Earl Brighton, my brother here may be involved in the church, but I do not see sainthood in his future."

"She's right. I'm fearful my feet will burn if I cross the threshold as of late," Aurélien said, adding in an ounce of mirth to pass off his truth as a joke. It worked with ease, the earl tossing back his head as he roared with laughter.

"What sins have you committed since your last confession, my good friend? Have you failed to fast during Lent?" Brighton asked, teasing.

Aurélien joined along in the laughter. "Oh, the usual—murder, torture, blasphemy."

"Oh, you've never sinned in your life, Saint-Orlant."

"From the way he haunted my confessional you'd think he was as guilty as they come," Celio remarked as he joined Aurélien's side. The devilspawn rolled his eyes.

"Father Celio, you would share my brother's dark secrets so easily?"

"I've taken a sabbatical from the church, no need to address me as such. The Church of Sanctuary is left in the most capable claws of Father Wren."

The conversation turned to simpler things with ease, fueled by the seemingly endless supply of liquor and opium smoke that hung low in the lounge many gathered in. White powders and snuff were taken in various ways and quantities by those within the Saint-Orlant townhouse: smoking, snorting, rubbing along the gums in drug addled fervor—none went as far as to produce vials of the drug's stronger counterparts to inject, but Aurélien hardly paid any in attendance much mind aside from his target. If the humans killed themselves with gluttony, he would only have a right laugh above their corpse and call upon a morgue to remove the rotting meat from his floors.

Aurélien partook in the revelry, rubbing cocaine along his gums and experiencing the slight thrill until his otherworldly blood burned away the intoxication in a matter of minutes. After the first two tastes, he didn't bother indulging unless presented to him on a silver tray by a guest. It would be rude for the host to refuse when so kindly offered. Still, as focused as he tried to be on the task at hand, his gaze wandered to Celio wherever he may be within the room. It was not simple protectiveness that kept him so transfixed upon the lilithspawn, but the innate desire to claim him before these unwilling witnesses. To mate before so many watchful eyes spoke of fertility and rituals of old.

Theia, to his surprise, was not aghast at the turn her once elegant soirée took. She lay upon one of the many occupied furnishings with who he believed to be Lady Marigold Thisld pressing her into the plush pillows, lost in each other's rouge painted lips. At her feet was Lady Marigold's husband, Lord

Frederick Thisld, kissing up her pale leg as though his wife was not there at all. They were hardly the first group to be lost in lust and ecstasy during this luscious gathering.

The finest women from The Orchid House danced in time to a drunk band, swaying their hips sensually. The women were arrayed in purple and scarlet color and decked with gold and precious stones and pearls. One danced towards Aurélien, a golden cup in her hand full of abominations and filthiness of her fornication, and pressed it into his hands. Aurélien recognized her as Myria, the two other women were no doubt her sisters. Without their habits and hidden behind glamours they were nearly unrecognizable.

"Quite the performance," Aurélien commented as Myria draped scarlet silk over his shoulder. Her breasts were bare, nipples perked in her excitement as moans flooded the room. Aurélien may have eyes only for Celio, but his gaze wandered from time to time—this was one of those moments. He longed, for but the beat of a hummingbird's heart, to bite into the flesh of her breast and hear her whine. Their dancing was an aphrodisiac, stronger than any wine, and the nobles and upper echelon were addicted.

"We are skilled. Us sisters take great pride in honing our mother's craft."

"Who is your mother, my dear?" Aurélien asked, drinking the liquid from her offered cup. It tasted like blood and wine mixed together with sin itself.

"Mystery, Babylon the Great! The mother of harlots and the abominations of the earth!" Myria said with glee, spinning on her heel to show Aurélien what her mother had gifted her, all the while quoting Revelations. Whether this was praise or mockery of her mother, he dare not guess. "We dance in her image—for the Whore of Babylon. And for you, our Dark Prince."

"She has blessed you well." Aurélien's gaze wandered until Celio came to stand beside her, arms crossed with a jealous look on his face.

"Would you mind repeating that, Little Love? I didn't quite hear."

"I was simply praising Myria on the gifts she received from the great Babylon. No need to be jealous."

"Jealous? I have every right to be jealous when some harlot is taking what is mine." Celio snapped his teeth in Myria's direction. She turned up her nose and left, making no fuss over the claim.

"Am I yours?" Aurélien asked with a pleased grin.

"I didn't say that… you're hearing things."

He could only grin wider, drawing the incubus in with a hand on the small of his back. "You did. You called me yours. Let me hear it again."

Celio scowled, pressed his hands against Aurélien's chest and attempted to get away. "Why do you need to hear what you already know? Fishing for compliments next?"

"Oh, are you giving out compliments next? These I must hear!" Aurélien grabbed a fistful of silky black hair and pulled Celio into a crushing kiss. Tonight, despite human society's standards, was about lust. Something as simple as gender was hardly going to bother them, not when so many were lost in sin themselves. Against teeth bitten lips, Aurélien growled, "Say I'm yours."

"You're mine and I am yours." Celio dove in for another kiss. They had hours to spend before they could move—what was a little pleasure to pass the time?

He Who Bleeds

Aurélien lifted Celio up, the lilithspawn wrapping his legs around his waist, and walked them to the nearest unoccupied wall. He pressed Celio's back against the warm elegantly carved marble of the fireplace's surround. The heat bothered neither demon as they tore away the clothing keeping them from feeling the press of each other's skin on their own.

Moaning filled the room, the human guests lost in the siren call of the Daughters of Babylon. It only fueled Celio's desire as he fed on the lust drenching the room. The orgy surrounding them held their attention very little, all that mattered was the taste of each other on their tongues.

Celio wriggled himself down from his perch, turning himself around and bracing himself against the mantle of the fire. His cock was hard, throbbing red when Aurélien glanced upon it while taking in the beautiful naked form of his lover. He turned and, with a devious smile, asked "Are you just going to stand there looking or are you going to fuck me like you hate me?"

Aurélien could only do as he commanded, caging Celio against the mantle and the roaring flames it held. He pressed his fingers between Celio's plump cheeks, rubbing small circles. "Should I stretch that pretty little hole of yours? Or do you want to cry on it?"

"Make it hurt," Celio instructed, pressing his hips back against the touch.

The last layers of clothes were shucked off and Aurélien spent a moment stroking his cock to fullness. "You are needy. Have I starved you?"

"Mhm, I'm—ah, starving!" Celio sang as Aurélien's cock entered him, tight walls clenching around his throbbing erection.

There was only passion in the way Aurélien fucked into his incubus, something as inconsequential as love was ignored. He laid his devotion onto Celio, every prayer and worship he could craft was presented to his false priest in the form of hard thrusts into his willing form. Energy buzzed across Aurélien's skin, his glamour flickering like a candle in the wind. Celio's glamour was in no better condition, unable to hide even his tail. It flickered in and out of sight with each hard thrust of his hips.

Precum sizzled on the fire as it dripped from Celio's aching cock, his moans nearly drowning it out as Aurélien pounded into him as though in heat. Aurélien craved every ounce of Celio and wished to feed on him as though he too was an incubus. Carnal pleasure fueled him when it was Celio.

"Do you like that, my pretty thing?" Aurélien asked, taking Celio's erection in hand. His lilithspawn whined, thrusting his hips pathetically into Aurélien's hand.

"Harder—harder… make it hurt. Make it *burn*."

A devilish grin spread across Aurélien's lips. "Naughty."

Aurélien pulled them down to the floor, a hand carefully placed so his lover wouldn't crumble onto the marble. Celio yelped, his fingers digging into the hot coals in the fire.

Fire didn't burn a demon's flesh. It only tingled and danced along the flesh like the mouth of an old lover, lapping up Celio's arm to welcome him.

"A-hh—hah—Little Love, like that. Just like that!" Celio screamed his adoration, dragging coals out of the fire. They rolled under Celio's chest, sizzling under his flesh.

Aurélien pressed him down onto the floor, fucking into him without regard for those in the room. He could feel eyes on his back, gawking, enjoying him for what he was—a monster.

They wouldn't remember this. Each of them had enough liquor in them to blur anything that happened that evening into a drunken dream.

"You were made to take me," Aurélien purred, taking in every whine and moan falling from Celio's mouth.

Celio palmed fruitlessly at his own cock, knowing better than to cum before being allowed. "My prince, oh I was made to be yours. Take me. Breed me. Create your spawn from me!"

Aurélien bent over him, his lips finding the soft tan skin of his back, leaving marks along his shoulders. He bit as he saw fit, tasting the drops of blood that sprung from beneath his fangs. The taste of him on his tongue made his thrust sputter, his orgasm building.

"Cum for me, Celio, let everyone hear how beautiful you are."

Celio cried out again, louder—arching his back into powerful thrusts that had both of them seeing stars. He spilled over the sprawling hot coals, whining Aurélien's pet names over and over.

Cum painted milky white streaks across Celio's back, mixing beautifully with the thin trail of blood that trickled down. Aurélien's breath was ragged as he pumped the last of his seed from his cock.

The sounds of the room came back to him quickly, the whines and moans from humans behind them were nothing compared to the pleas from his incubus. At that moment, he wanted for naught.

✝✝✝

Quiet was not how Aurélien would describe the early morning hours within his townhouse. Dawn had yet to fully come, sunlight barely tinting the London sky pale grey. A floor below the soirée still ran on, blue blooded aristocrats losing themselves in hedonism and lust fueled by copious amounts of opium, snuff and whatever else they could rub along their gums or smoke from a shared pipe.

What guest rooms he had were already claimed, leaving his parlor filled with guests too drunk to escort themselves home. Earl Jonathan Brighton was amongst the few men sleeping within the room, sitting upright on the armchair with a glass of brandy still clutched in his hand.

"Do you want me to do it?" Celio asked, an excited flint to his voice.

"No, I can do it. He is just a human." Aurélien allowed his glamour to fall, the crackle of Hellfire along his skin burned away his human facade. His tail whipped about with a mind of its own, excited to be free from its confines and glamour.

Celio shifted into the appearance of Brighton, drawing a knife from his waistcoat. "Can you really bear to kill your lover? Your boyhood love who fucked you so… badly? Is this what you liked so badly? Light skinned and blond and tall and fucking ugly?"

"Are you jealous of Brighton?" Aurélien asked, quirking a brow. He could feel the jealousy dripping from Celio despite the taunting expression on the false face of Brighton. "We had relations over a decade ago, there's no lost love. There never was *love*."

"I don't care if there was never love. Fucking *love*. You are mine. *Mine*. I do not like rotting festering humans coming to you with pleasant memories. You are mine. They should know that." Celio gestured to Brighton with the dagger. "Mine. I will kill him so his foul hands will never touch you again. You are mine to worship. Mine."

"Celio!" Aurélien barked. A man on the chesterfield stirred, giving them both pause until he was lulled back to sleep.

"I do not want to share," Celio spat, voice low.

"You're jealous of a dead man. Go. Go join the orgy below and give me an alibi. I will be finished soon."

Celio scowled, but dropped his glamour and slipped to the familiar one of Aurélien. The dagger was pressed into Aurélien's hand. "I'll be back when some pretty noble has licked my dick until he's sloppy."

The blade weighed heavy in his hand. He was left alone with their target and three other potential witnesses. It was hardly the easiest target to be given and having so much blood spilled in his own home was less than ideal—but this was the only way to do it without directly connecting him to the crime.

The first task was to end the witnesses, all drugged to a deep sleep-in thanks, at least partly, to the incense that burned in the room—the pints upon pints of brandy were another assurance that none within the room, even if awoken, would be able to stop what transpired. With the dagger in hand, Aurélien tilted the head of one of the witnesses back by a fistful of greasy hair. The edge pressed against the column of the man's throat, so sharp that blood beaded against the cool metal. Still, the man didn't stir and wouldn't until the knife cut into his throat to expose gurgling blood and rancid human meat. He woke, of course, as clawed fingers tore open his throat like a hungry beast might with its snout.

Dorian Valentine

There was a thrill to watching an animal bleed out under his knife. Aurélien found he rather enjoyed watching his targets squirm, gasp and plead with hollow eyes. A sliver of himself found it hard to believe that he enjoyed this—disgusted even. But, as he brought blood drenched fingers to his lips and licked them clean, the worried human still within quieted down as he tasted his prey.

Ecstasy was the only way he could describe the feeling that zipped through his body with each drop of blood he consumed. It made his nerves burn with barely laden Hellfire that burned in his core like an untamed inferno, coating his mind with only one thought: *more*. He should have been disgusted by what he did but instead he found pleasure in their pain. For someone who spent the entirety of his waking life as a human, he quickly adapted to his demonic tendencies. Such depraved thoughts didn't scare him, only spurred on his desire to create art. As he stood before his first kill of the night, that was all he saw. Art. These humans were his canvas to create with.

"Such a wasted opportunity," Aurélien said to himself, jabbing the dagger through the second witnesses' lower jaw, the long blade killing him instantly. After pulling the weapon free, Aurélien cupped his hands beneath his jaw, collecting blood in his palms. He drank it down like he would perish without it, energy buzzing about in his skin. Aurélien wasn't so far gone that he licked his hands clean, he had his mind about him as he gulped down the sweet blue blood of this noble.

The third man went as quickly, no struggle—no complaints, only gurgling as he choked on his own blood. This one Aurélien resisted tasting, his reputation within the back streets of London all but sullied the appeal of his blood. Aurélien ended his life with a quick stab through the heart, slotting the blade between ribs. It required no effort. None of these deaths did, hardly exciting him past the taste of their stolen blood.

Earl Jonathan Brighton still sat slumped in the armchair, unaware of the carnage before him or blood soaking into the Persian rug beneath Aurélien's feet. The devilspawn walked behind him, shoes sticking to the hardwood floor behind the chair.

"Many apologies, my good friend, but it was either me or you—and I am rather fond of myself. You understand, hm?"

Aurélien waited for a moment, as if expecting the drugged man to react to his statement. He didn't, only continued to dream. Despite the three deaths caused by his lilithspawn's dagger, it was still as sharp as a chirurgeon's scalpel. Aurélien pressed the blade against his neck, and with ease, cut through the flesh. It sliced through no different than butchering a hog, squelching as blood rushed forth. The pain woke Brighton, his body thrashing, and the start of a cry for help beginning before the knife cut through his neck entirely.

Rumors had it that the heads of those executed upon Charles-Henri Sanson's guillotine during the fabulously bloody French Revolution would blink and glare at their executioner. Aurélien was undeniably curious in regard to these old tales and, as he raised the removed head of his old friend before him with two hands like an offering to the gods, he felt rather disappointed. Brighton's removed head looked back at him, unmoving, slack jawed with unblinking dull eyes. So utterly boring.

Aurélien clicked his tongue, setting the head on the lap of the headless corpse. Where he typically felt excitement over a successful kill, he only felt disappointment. These four corpses were too easy. Too clean. Too boring. Gone was the chase, replaced with the unappealing drugged blue bloods on his chesterfield.

He swallowed and returned his glamour, slipping from the room to his own chambers while cloaked by shadows. The room was quiet, a perfect sanctuary. Aurélien cleaned his hands in a basin of water, tinging the water pink with the rapidly drying blood.

"Been busy?" Celio asked, appearing behind Aurélien in a gathering of shadows, shrugging off his glamour—the short blond hair of Brighton giving way for long black tresses.

Aurélien looked back at him through the mirror then began washing his face free of specks of blood. "Shouldn't you be pretending to be me?"

"I got bored. It's not the same without you."

"My alibi is important in this, darling."

Celio shrugged, removing the waistcoat from the devilspawn. "Wren stopped by and happily took over the helm while I, as Brighton, went to sleep off my drinks while you remained. A perfect alibi. You're about to be very popular—he has a wonderful tongue and adores using it, so many pleased noble men and women are about to testify to your location."

Aurélien turned to face him, eyes burning bright with that unshakable desire that refused to leave him alone since the moment he tasted blood. The false priest gasped, looking up at him in awe, his nude form trembling ever so slightly.

"By the Dark Lord's foul graces, you've been naughty, haven't you?" Celio cupped his cheeks in his warm hands. "You must be starving if you drank the blood of your kills. Little Love, come to me. Drink from me. You will feel better when my blood courses through you."

Aurélien looked down at him, hunger building within. His beautiful forsaken priest looked upon him with smiles and care he did not deserve. His skin glowed in the low lighting of his chambers, a delectable feast he wished to consume down to the bone. Perhaps further—the idea of sucking the marrow from Celio's delicate bones enticed him. Had he not lusted for him wholeheartedly, Aurélien would have done far worse than biting into the meat of his shoulder.

A devilspawn was many things, but an animal was not one of them. He did not tear with his teeth, dared not sample the meat so easily torn away—instead, he tasted. Aurélien drank a mouthful of the sweetest blood he had ever encountered, tinged with the tartness of berries. Celio pressed close, draping his arms around him as he allowed the unholy son to gorge himself on his ichor.

"Drink of me, my Dark Prince, consume me. I am but a vessel for your desires." Celio's cock was hard against Aurélien, and he couldn't deny his own stirred with cravings.

Another mouthful of blood was greedily stolen before Aurélien pulled away. He spent a moment lapping away the dribbles of blood, holding his prize by the small of his waist. "Your blood is delectable."

"No small praise coming from you," the incubus said, swooning both from the blood loss and his praise. "How did your task go then? Well? I haven't seen you so ravenous since you were young."

Aurélien sighed, dropping what little of his glamour remained. His tail drooped with his disappointment, tapping the floor with its own grievances. "Have I been known to fail?"

"Very true, Little Love—you are so magnificent you could not possibly fail at such an easy task. Tell me then, what made you so out of sorts?"

Fingers danced upon Aurélien's skin causing him to burn and tingle with his urges. The hunt hadn't been enough. It hadn't satisfied the devilspawn with its gore. Those worthless lives were worthless because they didn't possess the ability to become his art. They were as useless as an unwrapping party without the ancient corpse to unshroud from layer upon layer of fabric wrappings. "It was too easy. No hunt, no chase. Nothing but drunk men and their pathetic choking."

"How did you do it? Tell me," Celio instructed, a purr to his voice. He undid the buttons on Aurélien's shirt, peeling the blood speckled garment from him. With a glance, the garment burned away into ash in his hand—gone was any evidence that Aurélien had bathed in blood just moments before.

"I removed his head. He woke, tried to scream, but I had already cut through the vocal cords." Aurélien's fingers traced up the column of Celio's throat, feeling the tensing of his muscles beneath them. "And… so quickly did it end as your knife found its way through his spine. You know, I was half expecting to see him look at me. I expect Sanson had more fun than I did with such a disappointing victim."

"My love, the execution was beautiful—nothing you create is anything less than so. I dare anyone to question that."

"Nobody knows me as you do, Celio."

"I am yours. When Hell reaches up and consumes this rotten world with you at the helm, I shall be there at your side." Celio pressed kisses along his neck and chest, open mouthed and hot, working his way down.

He Who Bleeds

A sound not unlike a herd of cattle moved through the upper halls of Aurélien's townhouse, guests rushing past while speaking in rushed murmurs.

Wren appeared in the room cloaked in shadows, still donning Aurélien's face. "Quit fucking and get out there. Bodies have been discovered and I don't know the long game here."

Aurélien rolled his eyes, took quick stock of the way Wren wore his skin and allowed his human glamour to mimic the unkempt, post-coital appearance. "Celio, with me. Wren… just fuck off now."

"With pleasure," both incubi said. Wren flipped out of the window into the foggy London night and Celio dressed himself partially.

†Family Reunion†

A scream echoed through the townhouse, distinctly Theia's. Aurélien pushed through the crowd gathered before the scene of the crime in a frenzy, as any good older brother and host would do. Before him it was almost exactly as expected: the corpses were where he left them, and the scent of gore still hung in the air. The single difference infuriated him beyond reason. Upon their foreheads was a strange symbol carved with a sharp knife into the flesh.

Someone had defiled his creations. Had he been proud of the art he made, something as horrendous as a human's interference would send him into a violent rage. Upon closer inspection, he could see wounds he did not create—trophies no doubt taken from his kill. Unearned trophies.

"Someone send for Scotland Yard!" Aurélien commanded, reaching forward to gather Theia. She was shaking in his arms, sobs wrecking from her body as though these men meant anything to her.

A guest took off, he didn't care who just so long as this gathering ceased gawking at his failed creation. Celio pushed through the crowd, feigned disgust, and made the sign of the inverted cross.

"What devious things have happened beneath our very noses." A priest was someone the masses respected, even a half dressed retired one. Celio clapped his hands together in feigned prayer then turned around and waved for the crowd to leave. "Let us all make ourselves presentable and wait below for the Yard to arrive."

"Has anyone checked their pulses?" One gentleman called out, a medical student by the name of Anthony Gray. "Please, allow me."

Anthony Gray was a younger man in his mid-twenties, well dressed despite the thrills of the evening though his curly brown hair was mussed from the fingers of lovers. While those with unuseful education left at Celio's command.

The would-be doctor walked with a stumble that could only be brought about by excessive liquor. Gray looked around the room and, from a small table Aurélien often used to write letters, procured a pen.

"Do forgive me, old chap," Gray muttered, crouching before the corpse of one Earl Jonathn Brighton.

"Should we really be letting him do this?" Celio whispered, "I mean… what if he finds something?"

"What will he find?" Aurélien asked, raising an eyebrow. He watched the soon to be doctor putter around the room poking and prodding his creations with thinly veiled disgust and curiosity. "What news, doctor?"

"O-Oh I'm no doctor yet, but I'll do in a pinch. These men were killed within the last two hours."

"I saw Brighton not too long ago—these other men, I'm not sure. Anything else?"

Gray swallowed, standing up. "I wouldn't know until I examined further, and I need not remind you that I am underqualified for this. We best wait for the Yard to arrive. But it looks as though each had… something removed."

"Like a head?" Celio asked, trying to hide his amusement by looking away.

"Well, yes, but more than that. It appears Brighton had his eyes removed after the fact. Beaufort has had his nails removed. Sheffield had his oesophagus cut out after being… well it looks like it was torn open—" Gray pressed the back of his wrist to his mouth, gagging. "Torn open by something. And Greville here was stabbed through the jaw. I don't know what was taken from him, if anything at all."

"Scotland Yard, sir." Oscar lingered at the doorway, flagged by two constables and a man most certainly an inspector, judging by the dark circles under his eyes which spoke of being roused from his sleep for this. Whether the Yard was always so quick to rush to the scene of a crime or if their hurry spoke only of the location of the crime, Aurélien couldn't say. He would lean towards the latter, if he was a betting man.

"Good evening, gentlemen. We are most appreciative of your quick arrival."

"I am Inspector Holloway of Scotland Yard. Are you the proprietor of this townhouse, Mr…?" The inspector, despite his Yorkshire accent and definitively English surname, sported short cropped red hair and muted green eyes.

"Saint-Orlant," Aurélien supplied, standing aside to allow the inspector and his group of constables to enter. Evidently, whomever made the frantic run to the Yard had not given adequate details on the situation. The devilspawn hid his grin well as he watched even the seasoned inspector gag at the display.

"Simply barbaric," the inspector commented. "Miller, return to the Yard and fetch six more constables and the coroner.

West, see that none leave and none enter until we have backup. I need everyone's comings and goings known, even the mice."

The constables nodded their affirmation and departed for their duties. Inspector Holloway turned back towards Aurélien. "This is a right bloody mess. Has anyone touched the bodies?"

"I have. I checked for pulses on the… more intact victims," Gray informed.

"And you are?" Inspector Holloway asked, flicking open a notebook.

"Anthony Gray. I'm a medical student at the Royal College of Surgeons. Under Doctor Tolland, sir."

Inspector Holloway made a noise of interest. "Can any of you positively identify the victims before us?"

"Jonathan Brighton. Edgar Sheffield. Marion Beaufort. Cornelius Greville. They were all friends in some way or another. Hadn't seen any of them in some time, but we were all lost in our own worlds. Too much liquor." Aurélien feigned sadness, teetering on the shakiness of held back emotions and the masculinity of a man trying to appear strong in the face of horror.

"And you are, sir?"

Celio had been praying since they heard the footsteps down the hall signaling the arrival of company. They were, of course, false prayers damning these men's souls to Hell in offering to the Dark Lord. When spoken to, his muttering ceased. "I am Father—just Celio Beausoliel."

"Why the correction?" the inspector asked, raising a brow.

"I've recently left the church—a sabbatical, if you will. The Church of Sanctuary is in the capable hands of my deacon, not to worry. I wanted to experience the world before entirely devoting my life to the Lord."

"I've heard talk about that church. Strange place. Unorthodox."

"All is good in the eyes of our Lord. Any worship is accepted, all love is taken with appreciation." Celio smiled, and where one devout to God would raise their hands in gesture to the Heavens, his hands gestured to the floor below. It was a small act that anyone would easily dismiss as the priest being flippant, but Aurélien recognized it for worship of the Dark Lord. Briefly he wondered if he would ever meet the man who brought him life, born from His unholy flesh.

Inspector Holloway nodded. "Mr. Saint-Orlant, can you provide a list of all guests in attendance as well as all your servants—long-term and temporary?"

"For the most part. My sister, Theia Saint-Orlant, was in charge of the invitations, not to mention whoever decided to come uninvited. I'll gather the information from her and have a servant deliver it to Scotland Yard upon completion." Aurélien paused, glancing at the bodies, then dipped his head down. "If you'll excuse me. I… I need to pray for their souls. These were good men. They didn't deserve this… this vile dismemberment."

Aurélien left the room before Inspector Holloway could object, quickly followed by Celio and Oscar. Sanctuary, when one's home was being torn apart by the Yard, was a hard thing to find, as it turns out. As he pushed into his thankfully empty bedrooms with a pair of loyal followers in tow, Aurélien only ached for the safety of The Church of Sanctuary.

By now, of course, he knew the church was not one to the Catholic God, but to the Dark Lord. Each prayer said corrupted and twisted before unknowing patrons who pressed meager coins into the offering plates handed out by demons. It had not always been so—at one point, before Celio drew it away from the Englishman's God, it had been a perfectly respectable place of worship.

"A right mess you lot have made here," Oscar scolded, cursing under his breath again before raking his hand down his face.

"I'm afraid I don't know what you mean, Oscar." Aurélien sat at the small table he oft ate breakfast at, pinching the bridge of his nose between his fingers. Oscar was right—this was a bloody mess.

"Thirty Heaven-damned years down the fucking drain," he continued on, rolling his neck side to side to further expel tension. With the motion, a gauze-like glamour peeled itself from his skin. Celio had informed him once that the Dark Lord's spawn retained a majority of their beauty when in their true form. For Aurélien this meant aside from the tone of his skin turning to the paleness of a corpse, something many in such a cloudy city could overlook, and the appendages which sprouted forth, he was as handsome as *Le génie du mal*. The same seemed to apply to Oscar as well—for if Aurélien was *Le génie du mal,* Oscar was *L'ange du mal*. The devilspawn before him possessed skin the color of Mediterranean clay, long dark hair poured to the hardwood floor beneath his feet, dragging behind him as he stepped forward. It turned to thick black smoke at the ends, the smothering of a roaring inferno that somehow lingered that the very ends of his hair. Like Aurélien, he possessed horns that arched backwards, wings the color of a starless night and, no doubt trapped beneath the servant Oscar's clothing, a tail.

This stunned Aurélien more than he'd ever care to admit, but what froze him entirely in his place was the confused, frightened look upon Celio's delicate face. "Y-you?"

Blood recognized blood. Something stirred in him, and he knew his answer. Before Oscar could open his mouth again, Aurélien answered. "My brother."

"So, you do know how to recognize your betters. Good. I had my worries after learning Father left his favorite harlot in charge of your care." Oscar flashed a sharp grin in Celio's direction. The incubus drew in onto himself, clearly wanting to hide away from the demon before him. "I am Axædus. I presume you've heard of me."

"Commander of thirty legions. Second son of the Dark Lord." Celio added in a voice much smaller than Aurélien had ever heard.

Axædus simply smiled and preened under the quivering praise like a true coxcomb. "At your service, little imp, very much at your service. Dear old Father asked me to come check on you."

"The Dark Lord asked about me Himself?" the devilspawn asked, breathlessly.

A brow rose on Axædus' beautiful face. "You needn't call Him so—subserviently. Father is just Father."

"Why has His Highness asked of us?" Celio asked.

"Silence, harlot—the real demons are talking here." Axædus raised a pair of fingers to Celio, and without even turning to look upon him, silenced him. Celio's lips screwed up and he whined, attempting to tear apart his fused together mouth. Axædus sighed, grinding his heel into the floor while he gathered himself. "We all felt the contract begin to break. Whatever this *moron* did, he failed to fully destroy the thing. If we in Hell felt it, so did your owner, dear brother."

"Why are you talking about Celio like that?" Aurélien asked. He hated the way his so-called brother was talking about his lilithspawn. He hated that unctuous expression on his face. There was nothing he wanted more than to punch it off of Axædus.

"Don't tell me you sympathize with—"

"Undo whatever in God's name you did to him." A zip of pain ran through Aurélien's body as he spoke God's name. Punishment—but from which divine side he couldn't be sure.

Axædus rolled his eyes—a pale blue, nearly white in a distinctly inhuman way. With a snap of his fingers, Celio was gasping for air, rubbing his sore lips, and scowling at the demon. "Weak little brother doting on Father's used whore. We have more important matters to worry about. Like the blood bath you've created in your own home and the unbroken contract."

"I'm working on it." Aurélien looked at the door just past his supposed brother. "Have you… always been Oscar? Or should I expect my valet to fall from a closet dead?"

"Worried about a human too? How far you must climb to reach glory now, brother. This Oscar he… is alive. I left him in the capable hands of Az. If the sex hasn't killed him, he'll be returning a very happy man soon enough. Az sends his regards, by the way. He's quite excited to meet his newest nephew."

An inquisitive look must have passed over Aurélien's face as Celio leaned close and whispered. "Demon of lust, one of the kings of Hell. You know this—he was an angel like the Dark Lord."

Axædus clicked his forked tongue. "I need to keep reminding myself you're a clueless little welp. So, can I be assured you two imbeciles have a plan?"

"I did—I do. That graceless barbarian has defiled my art—taken parts of it. Under my own nose. How he—"

"Oh, for the love of—" Axædus groaned. "Nobody cares about your 'art', brother. Art can matter when you've established a following. Need I remind you that at present you only have only a handful of whores? Tell me, have you even figured out who holds the contract?"

"My father," Aurélien spat.

The Second General of Hell clapped his hands in a slow and patronizing way. "Wow, he is good. He's cracked the case dear Celio, your help has truly paid off! Let us rush home and tell everyone that little Celio has saved the day."

"His *human* father," Celio growled, shrugging off the heavy arm that Axædus draped over his shoulder.

"Hmm? Hm. Now that is a fun twist, isn't it?"

"*Fun* is not how I'd describe my eternal servitude."

Another click of a tongue. "Well, Father has asked me to put an end to all of this. I can either do this the easy way: you make a contract with me to kill your owner, or the hard way: I help just enough to see that you don't land yourself at the noose. Because honestly, we don't need people finding out demons are walking amongst them."

"What would this contract entail?" Aurélien asked after a moment considering what lay before him. A contract with Axædus seemed to be the easiest way out, but he had no idea what the devilspawn would ask for in exchange for his services. The grin spreading over Axædus' handsome features unsettled him and Aurélien decided before the words even left his serpent's mouth to not agree.

"Nothing much. Just the life of your favorite little incubus. A life for a life and all that."

"No."

"In death there will be mercy. Think of your freedom. You would give it all up for—for *it?*" The disgust twisted off of Axædus' tongue and around the word *it*. Like Celio was less than. Unworthy of even being recognized as another demon. "It will be a liability when you return to Hell. It will be used against you, this weakness of yours. I could see it the moment I came to this plane, and I know I am not the only one who sees."

Axædus paused, furrowing his brow as he looked at the pair before him. "Not all of our kin are as magnanimous as I— many would desire your death. Would you so easily give them the upper hand?"

"Who I bed with is none of your concern," Aurélien hissed. "I appreciate your… generous offer, Ax—"

His mouth screwed up painfully, stinging like it had been sewn shut with a dull needle.

Axædus' laughter filled the room, a wide, devilish grin on his face. "Look at you! So confused. Has your oh so wonderful teacher not told you? Lesser demons cannot say the name of their betters without permission and you, little brother, do not. Aurélien—I am your better. Remember that."

The devilspawn rushed forward, taking Aurélien's jaw in his clawed hand. "I will return in three days. Think it over. Fuck it out. I don't care how, but know this—I do not disappoint Father."

Pointed claws dug into his flesh, pin pricks of hot black blood beaded out beneath the nails before Axædus removed his hair. He smiled a pleased, all-knowing smile that Aurélien couldn't quite place, then left. His body melted before their eyes, soaking into the wooden floor, slipping through cracks and crevices to drip back into Hell.

Celio, who had sat like he was pinned in place, stood, and rushed to Aurélien's side with a handkerchief in hand. He dabbed away the blood on the devilspawn's jaw. "I should've known one of your brothers would eventually show up. But why did it have to be *him*?"

"Ax—" he paused, feeling the pricks along his tongue as he went to speak his brother's full name. "Ax will not lay a single finger on you."

The lilithspawn's face was twisted with a sad, pained sort of smile. He didn't share the sentiment, clearly. "Little Love, I think you should accept his deal."

"Cast the very idea from your mind, Celio. I will never take his Heaven-damned deal so long as I live." Aurélien drew Celio in tight. In that moment he realized he had never held Celio so close, at least, not outside the heats of passion. He felt the incubus tense up at the touch then melt into him, pressing his face into his chest for comfort.

It occurred to Aurélien that Celio was afraid of Axædus. Even he was wary of the man; the powerful, proud aura surrounding his older brother spoke of his strength—of how easily Axædus could destroy them both with a single glance. There was a terror coursing through his smaller form, shaking ever so slightly. Aurélien was unaware that demons could even feel fear, but he considered that perhaps incubi were different in that regard.

"Why… don't you hand me over? Anyone else would. I'm *just* an incubus. There's plenty of us. You won't even miss me. Someone better will come, someone more beautiful. Probably someone worthy of you. Not like me." Sniveling was not something he expected from Celio. He had seen him cry, of course, when lost in the throes of passion but this was different. It set him on edge in a new way, tensing fully as he gently rubbed his back.

"Nobody could replace you."

"I've heard that before…" Celio muttered. His voice was muffled by the barely buttoned shirt Aurélien wore.

Aurélien knew, despite only a brief encounter with his demonic brother, that very little of what he said could be trusted. Not trusting a demon was a lesson many knew, though at the time it was a superstition as true as the threat of being sent off to work in the coal mines if he didn't finish his breakfast. He wondered briefly if such scheming and lying told through stories applied to fellow demons or better yet, to demonic kin. "Whoever told you that was as stupid as they were blind. You are exquisite, Celio, such a brilliant little incubus. Without you I would be lost in all of this—or worse, still split between myself."

"It was your father, the Dark Lord. I disappointed Him. Keeping an eye on you was a punishment. Staying in that church where my feet burned for years was my punishment for insulting His grace."

"Do you still consider this a punishment?" Aurélien asked, hooking a finger under Celio's jaw. He tilted his head up. Celio looked rather handsome with tear-stained cheeks. "Have I not treated you perfectly? My consort and lover. Do I not fuck you well enough? If not, I will have to be twice as demanding to convince you."

Celio suddenly laughed, snorting—startling himself. "You have long since ceased being my punishment. You are my passion, my Dark Prince. My reason for living."

Aurélien captured his lips in a kiss, not caring for the click of their teeth together or the cuts their fangs made upon one another. "I do have one question."

"Ask it, Little Love." Celio clung to him, his tears already replaced with a soft smile.

"Am I a better lover than the Dark Lord?"

Celio laughed again, grinning now. He walked his fingers up Aurélien's chest. "You are. I've never had a lover so vigorous or so… gifted."

"Not even Him?"

The smugness was heard in Celio's voice. "Not even Him. You are *oh* so perfect. When I am with you, I am filled. I am satiated. I want for nothing."

A knock came, and with regret, Aurélien pulled himself away from Celio to answer it. On the other side was Inspector Holloway, looking as weary as Aurélien himself felt.

"Any headway, Inspector?" Aurélien asked, feigning interest. It was quite hard to be interested in a case one knew more intimately than anyone within the Yard could ever dream of.

Inspector Holloway raised a brow, glancing behind Aurélien at the priest with tear-stained cheeks. "Not as far as we would hope. My team has gathered all the intel needed from the guests here."

"That's excellent news."

The human coughed awkwardly. "In the interest of keeping this case as clear cut as possible, I am willing to ignore several broken laws at this gathering of yours, Lord Saint-Orlant."

Aurélien hummed inquisitively. "Hm? And what laws would that be?"

"Judging by witness testimony—adultery, sodomy, incest—just to name a few."

His smile dropped, turning into a sneer. "Are you attempting to black mail me, Inspector?"

A wave of a hand. "Not at all. I simply wish to come to an understanding. You will ensure you are the most forthcoming with information and I won't let slip to the papers the interesting gossip we've uncovered."

"So, black mail."

"Call it what you will, Lord Saint-Orlant. Do have yourself a wonderful rest of your night. And please, don't forget the list of guests you promised—we would hate to miss even a single possible suspect." Inspector Holloway tipped his head and made his way back down the hall towards the stairs—evidently done with his work for the night.

Aurélien slammed the door behind him, cursing under his breath. He hated these humans and their rules and regulations. When forced to step away from human society he saw how foolish all of it was. How quickly he discarded the life he once lived.

Despite how much he hated it, he had to play their game. Just for a little longer. As Celio came to his side offering soothing touches, Aurélien only seethed in his anger.

He must kill his father. He must destroy Baron Montague Edwin Saint-Orlant before playing human finally kills him.

†Gunpowder†

Theia paced around the dining room that morning, her house shoes clicking about in a rhythmic tone that Aurélien would almost call soothing had she not been wrecked with fright and nerves he didn't quite understand. He watched helplessly, not that he was inclined to help, as she wore away at his hardwoods with her heels and ignored the chilling breakfast on the table.

The devilspawn held no such reservations, eating his breakfast with the practiced manners of high society. Celio sat beside him, tracing his fingers along his inner thigh to beg for his own breakfast. Aurélien decided his lilithspawn was becoming more insatiable and it needed to be quelled soon.

"I-I just don't understand. How could this happen right under everyone's noses? Not a single scream? Nothing! Oh, and now that inspector from Scotland Yard *knows* what we all did. What we both did. Aurélien, how can you sit there and eat when that man has enough evidence to throw us all in prison?" Theia slapped her hand down onto the table, rattling the delicate China.

Aurélien glanced up at her then picked up his tea, drinking slowly to make a point. "Inspector Holloway and I have an arrangement. So long as I remain cooperative in the Yard's investigation, he will refrain from mentioning my sin of sodomy. Not to mention adultery and so forth."

"The cheek of that man! Black mailing the Saint-Orlant family."

He Who Bleeds

"Little Love, I can't help but think this is partially my fault." Celio pouted, batting long lashes at Aurélien. It worked to distract him, but only for a moment.

"What would Father think if he learned of this," Theia wailed, wrapping thin arms around herself as she shook with her own anxieties.

Aurélien sighed, looking over his sister. Briefly he wondered if she too was like Oscar—hidden away and replaced with another devilspawn to watch over him. "I don't particularly care what that man thinks of me. Rotten bastard."

"Aurélien! How could you say that about Father?"

The incubus laughed, propping his head up in his hands. "How naughty of you, Lord Saint-Orlant!"

Aurélien felt right drawn thin, his frustration bubbling up as he tried to separate the two sides of his being. It was tiring, exhausting even, to wear a glamour inside his own home, to be the perfect son, the perfect host. To be something he no longer was and wasn't sure if he ever had been. Aurélien breathed in deeply then exhaled, allowing his glamour to flicker away. He was so damn tired.

Rising from his seat, rage boiled at the borderline kind words Theia spoke about that pathetic sack of meat and gas. He snarled his words, voice louder than anticipated. "I don't care what that man would think. After everything he's done to me. He made me the way I am. He is no father to me. The baron will be nothing but waste under my boot when I'm done with him."

No scream erupted from Theia's lips like he expected. She only stared; eyes wide with her hands clutched to her chest. Stepping backwards, without taking her eyes off of Aurélien, she asked, "What did you do to my brother? What are you? Who are you?"

"Don't scare the mortal, Little Love. They get strange when they're scared." Celio's hands were on his shoulders, coaxing his wings to return into hiding. His own glamour fell, his beautiful lilithspawn replacing the well-presented priest.

"You're acting like a starved feline. Do I not feed you enough?" Aurélien drew Celio in for a kiss, letting him take just a taste. When he was finished, he turned his attention to the quaking mortal he once called sister. "I am Aurélien, son of the Dark Lord. I have never been mortal. Not once. Not when we played in the fields around the manor. Not when your father wed your mother. The demon lurked there, waited—until Celio freed me."

"Why would… why would a p-priest serve the devil?" Her voice shook. Theia was afraid and Aurélien lavished in that terror.

"Not a priest, darling, just an incubus with *hunger*. I do look rather nice in the vestments, though. Who knew priests could be so *desirable*?" Celio sat himself on the table, attempting to guide Aurélien in between his legs with a pull of his tail.

"W-what does this have to do w-with Father? Our father was kind to us. Stern, but kind. Why… why do you speak as though—"

"Because he *made* me. He created me to be his assassin. I have killed countless for him to rise in his ranks. Competition. Enemies. Heavens, those who spit at his feet by accident. None have been free from my blade because he commanded it. The baron will die and either you stay out of my way, or you can die with him."

Theia was a Saint-Orlant through and through. She swallowed and stepped forward until she was just a step away from the demons. "If I help you, will you grant me a wish?"

Celio clapped his hands excitedly. "Your first contract! Oh, Little Love, how exciting!"

A twinge of confusion passed through Aurélien. He shouldn't be shocked, but he found himself to be utterly so. He knew disgustingly well about demons and their contracts, but to take on one of his own was beyond his imagination. In fact, it had never crossed his mind outside the ramblings of Celio during their missions together. Yet as a contract presented itself unto him, it sounded downright alluring. "What is it that you wish for? What would you bind yourself to the devil's scion so readily for?"

The mortal took a slow breath, her hand moving to grasp her stomach in a way that almost assured Aurélien that her next words would be asking for immaculate conception. "I want to be a man. I want to look like who I feel on the inside. I want Theia to die and everyone to remember me as Theodore, as Theo. If you do this… if you can make me who I want to be, I will help you kill our father."

"You are truly a Saint-Orlant. Bargaining whenever you can. Scheming. Always getting your desires. It's why I've always liked you, brother." Aurélien snapped his fingers on instinct, a contract appearing in his hand with their terms drawn up. "Celio, please help my brother with a glamour. I want to know I have this inner man *perfect*."

"Just like that?" Theo asked. He looked stunned, but after a moment his shoulders relaxed.

Celio conjured a mirror and sat it before Theo, making him sit at the table. "So, tell me—how big do you want it?"

"How big do I want what?"

The incubus only laughed and began crafting the perfect glamour, tweaking it here and there according to Theo's direction until it was exactly as he wanted. The man looked partly the same, like a brother to the woman who once was but never really was. His blond hair was shortened, cherub like curls falling just past his ears. His jaw was sharper, nose a little different and overall, a much more masculine look. Gone was his chest and the gown he had worn was replaced with a masculine cut. Theo was still a feminine man, but now it was the kind many women would swoon over, having a gentle air about him. A smile stretched across his lips as he studied himself, tears flowing down his cheeks. "Is that... me? Really and truly me?"

Celio nodded his head. "You are exquisite, Monsieur Saint-Orlant."

Theo stood, wobbling with the new height, and took a step back to look over everything. His face flushed slightly, coughing away some embarrassment. "It will take a little time to get used to *that*."

"Our contract is ready to be signed, Theo. Are you pleased with the glamour? It will become permanent once our signatures are down." Aurélien picked up a knife from the table, wiping it with a napkin. He walked to his brother's side, and even with Theo's new height, Aurélien towered over him a good head.

"It's perfect," he assured, touching his face again as if it would slip away.

Celio hopped up onto the table, crossing his legs while he held the unsigned contract. "May I say your name, Little Love?"

Aurélien nodded his head. "You always can."

He Who Bleeds

The lilithspawn grinned in response and began reciting the contract's most basic terms. "This contact hereby binds the Dark Prince Aurélien, son of the Morning Star, ruler of thirteen legions in Hell, general in His Infernal Army to the mortal Theia Vivienne Saint-Orlant. Terms are as follows: the demon Aurélien shall replace all memories in mortals of Theia Vivienne Saint-Orlant with his new identity—Theodore Montague Saint-Orlant—which he shall henceforth be referred to as such. His current glamour shall become permanent and replace any and all female associated attributes upon signing of this infernal contract. In exchange, Theodore Montague Saint-Orlant shall assist in the termination of the contract between Baron Montague Edwin Saint-Orlant and the demon Aurélien. In the event that Aurélien passes before the contract is complete, all associated terms will be considered complete and Theodore Montague Saint-Orlant will retain the benefits of this contract."

Aurélien brought the knife to his palm, the blade cutting into the flesh making black blood bubble up from underneath his pale skin. Celio handed over an ink dip pen, his smile unfaltering.

The demon handed the knife to his human brother then dipped the pen into the pooling blood in his cupped palm. With it, he signed the contract.

Theo brought the knife to his left palm, hesitating for a moment before cutting into the flesh. He hissed and dropped the blade, red blood pooling quickly from the too deep cut. He took the pen from Aurélien and signed his name just below his with his own blood.

Fire danced from the contract up Theo's arm, coating his entire being in a flash—forming, molding, creating the new him. An agonized groan came from him, a cut off scream that he silenced with a bloody palm as he fell to his knees as each bone in his body reformed into its new shape. In a moment it was all over—a lifetime's amount of ache pushed through.

Theo's breath was ragged as he hauled himself to his shaky feet. He produced a handkerchief and wrapped it around his bloodied palm. "Thank you, Aurélien... I-I need a day, possibly two, to adjust to this new me, but when the time comes, I am in your debt. Whatever I must do, I will do."

The devilspawn held his bleeding hand out to Celio expectantly. Celio's eyes lit up and he held the wounded hand as delicately as an injured bird. Tentatively he leaned down and licked the wound, pushing over the meat in a way that should not have been so pleasurable. Aurélien swallowed his moan, pushing through the desire that burst forth in part due to the aphrodisiac properties of incubus spit. Celio lapped at the cut as though it were a noblewoman's cunt, tasting every drop of blood that pooled on the tongue until it healed. When he finished, he licked the healed wound twice, then his lips and whined for more.

"Take all the time you need." Aurélien gently patted Celio's cheek.

Theo's face was flushed even deeper, watching the perverted display with disgust and fascination. "What... was that?"

"Hmm?" Celio's inquisitive hum was floaty, high on the devilspawn's blood.

"My trickster priest here is an incubus. One I fear I spoiled like a house cat."

"A house cat that should be tossed in a bag and thrown into the River Thames." A smokey, sulphuric smell permeated the room. Hellfire shrouded the voice's owner for an instant. Axædus' heels clicked on the floor. He was dressed elegantly, not in the drab clothing of a servant this time—cutting a slim and regal image in dark reds, gold and black. His shirt was sheer silk, the color of old blood and left nothing to the imagination. The same could be said for the leather trousers he wore, skintight as though painted on—though these were barely visible, covered by heeled boots that lace up entirely to his thighs.

"I told you to fuck off, didn't I?"

Axædus clicked his tongue, shaking his head. "Oh, how cruel. I only wished to come congratulate my littlest brother on his *very* first contract. I remember my first, Father was so proud of the destruction it brought. Yours is… cute."

"Leave, Ax, I don't need your help in this matter. I will not reconsider."

"I was just in the area. Besides, Father asked me to pass along a gift." Axædus tossed something to Aurélien, which he caught easily. It was a small metal cube, silver in color, and weighed a good amount. "Your weapon, dear brother. Name it, sculpt it—it'll always be yours."

Aurélien turned it over in his hand. He saw nothing of interest, only smooth metal on all sides. "How can this be a weapon?"

"You could throw it really hard," Theo suggested, nervously. His eyes hadn't left Axædus since the demon entered the room.

"Cheeky little mortal." Axædus laughed. With a twist of his hand, he summoned forth a whip made of the same metal as the cube. "It forms to your will, brother. Our weapons are made from the only substance that can injure a heavenly body. Infused with the essence of Father's torn away wings. Very potent. Commune with it, it shall answer. We are, after all, nearly perfect copies of Father."

Communicating with a hunk of metal was an odd suggestion, but he had little reason not to believe his brother. Comments regarding the lilithspawn aside, he hadn't done anything to suggest he was untrustworthy in that regard. Though, after a minute or two of staring at the cube, he decided it was a lie—that is until it began shaking in his palm.

"Just like that," Axædus praised, walking closer to observe, his chain whip dragging on the floor behind him.

The strange metal melted quickly, like it had been in the fires of the underworld. Aurélien cupped it with two hands, watching it boil—shaping and forming itself into its final form. It didn't burn like true molten metal would. It didn't eat away at his flesh or singe. When it finished boiling away, Aurélien was left with a gun. Not unlike a pistol, though its barrel was longer and rather rectangular in shape.

"My, my," Axædus said in amazement, leaning forward for a better look.

The gun fit nicely into Aurélien's hand—a perfect weight. It felt right in his grip, sculpted just for him. He opened the clip and found that it was filled with silver bullets. "It's a little inconvenient that I will have to carry my own ammunition."

Axædus rolled his eyes. "It reloads itself. Mortal made bullets would be useless in such a creation."

"It's beautiful, Little Love. You look very rugged with it," Celio assured, feeling his bicep to make a point.

"So, this weapon can kill heavenly bodies?"

"As long as you're not a shit shot," Axædus said, looking over his claws without a care. They were needle sharp, stained black at the tips. Despite the nonchalant stance, Aurélien knew he was aware of his surroundings. If Axædus was truly a general and son of the Dark Lord, as claimed, he would be on guard at all times. That didn't matter to Aurélien. With this new weapon he could be rid of this annoying kin.

Aurélien raised the gun. There was no reloading, no pouring of gunpowder, not even a hammer to draw back. Only the pull of the trigger. There was hardly any recoil as he pulled it. Once. Twice, for good measure. The sound rang and the scent of gunpowder filled the air.

Axædus grinned despite the twin bullets entering his body, hardly even moving a step back as the impact jostled him. The devilspawn groaned, black blood rising to the wounds before closing. Not even his clothing retained their wounds. Axædus leaned forward and retched into his open palms, coughing up the two bullets. He handed them back to Aurélien, wet with his saliva and blood. "You should aim higher, Aurélien."

"Should I try again? I need target practice and who better than you?" Aurélien asked, holding his gun steady. He dropped the bullets he was handed. They clattered on the floor.

"We'll have to see which is faster. My whip or your pistol." Axædus smiled so wide his skin stretched to nearly breaking, his sharp teeth on display. "So, put that thing down and we'll put this tantrum behind us."

Aurélien kept his gaze on his brother, watching him as he lowered his gun.

"Good boy. I knew you were smart. Smarter than Xerxes, at least." The whip in Axædus' hand disappeared again and he turned his attention to Theo. "Is it really such a good idea to have a mortal around? Even one so handsome."

"Leave him alone."

"Now, now, I'm just trying to have a conversation. What is your name, mortal? I know you can speak."

Theo looked up at Axædus with wide, starry eyes. "Theodore Saint-Orlant."

"Saint-Orlant! Why, is this one from last night? Mh—you might not recognize me out of that disgusting meat suit you lot called Oscar, but I remember you. Your taste," Axædus purred, cupping Theo's cheeks with clawed hands.

"T-That was you?" Theo stuttered out, cheeks flushing.

Celio scowled, crossing his arms. "He curses us lilithspawn and then whores himself out."

"Such disdain for your betters, incubus." Axædus shook his head. A hand was placed on the small of Theo's waist, pulling him in until their bodies were pressed together. The mortal's face flushed even more. "Will you allow me to assist in learning your new form, Theodore? I can assure my tongues are even more exciting on male anatomy."

"I-I… ummm."

"Just nod your head, mortal."

Theo nodded his head quickly.

Aurélien grabbed his brother's hand and pulled it away from Theo, holding his wrist tight. "You are not fucking him. Leave. You're not getting a contract lurking about my manor."

Axædus huffed. "You are an idiot to not accept my help. With my help, it could be over in an instant. Just kill the bitch and you will be free. No need to dirty the hands of this fine man."

"Take the deal, Little Love." Celio's voice was small, laced with terror, not unlike the night before when he was chastised by

Axædus. Aurélien swallowed, glancing between his incubus and demonic brother.

"Well, it seems you do have worthwhile thoughts in that cockbrain of yours. Perhaps that's why Father kept you around." Axædus looked Celio up and down. "Though I doubt it."

"I'm not killing you, Celio. You're not some pawn."

"You're so *witless*. I take back what I said before. You're even more moronic than Xerxes. All muscles, no brains." Axædus laughed, yanking his hand away. "I could save you. I could *free* you, yet you insist on ignoring my good gesture."

"Shall I shoot you again?"

"A waste of perfectly good bullets." A mischievous grin spread over his face again, wide, and eerie.

"You can't ask my brother to kill the man he loves! That's downright monstrous." Theo slipped himself from Axædus's embrace, scowling at the demon like he had any authority over this creature from Hell.

Axædus stared for a second then barked a laugh, loud and roaring like he had heard the funniest joke in all the lands. "Demons cannot feel something as human as *love*. That is why we are better in every aspect! Love. *Love*—ah, how silly."

Celio ducked his head in shame, stepping back to create more space between himself and the higher up demons.

A gentle knock came from the door, a soft voice coming through. "Lord Saint-Orlant, an inspector from Scotland Yard is here to see you."

Aurélien didn't take his eyes off his brother, slipping on his human glamour once again. Warm and familiar like a well-worn pair of shoes. "Thank you, Dorcus."

†Human Curiosity†

Inspector Holloway stood within a large parlor where, just hours before, a roaring orgy occurred. He admired the paintings on the walls, old things with yellowing varnish from decades' worth of smoke from the hearth and cigars. The scent of sex still faintly lingered, undetectable to a human's nose. Two constables were also within the room, taking in the art and decor—whether or not they were searching for some secret within the art Aurélien couldn't say.

"Inspector Holloway, I wasn't expecting your return so soon. Have you had a break in the case already?" Aurélien asked, stopping by a small table cluttered with crystal cut decanters of various strong liquors. He poured himself two fingers of strong bourbon, raising a brow in an offering motion towards the inspector.

"No, thank you, Lord Saint-Orlant. I remain on duty, as it were." Inspector Holloway strode across the room, closer to Aurélien than he would have liked. "I intend to thoroughly investigate the room in question once more. The coroner has come back with his report and the corpses were perplexing to say the least."

"How so?" Aurélien asked, curiously. He'd be a fool not to want to hear a professional's review on his art—even art tainted by some filthy mortal.

"It goes against an exorbitant amount of rules to even discuss the findings with you, Lord Saint-Orlant. You can find out through the broadsheets."

Aurélien sipped his bourbon. It went down smooth like butter on a hot pan. "You've already black mailed me, Inspector Holloway, I won't speak this to anyone. I have a right to know what was done under my own nose, do I not?"

"Rather early in the day for liquor, isn't it?"

"Mh. Long night. I'm sure you understand." Aurélien smiled faintly at his own lie drenched statement.

Inspector Holloway made a sound of agreement that said he too would be drinking if he was in Aurélien's position. "Right. Each man died a unique death. Furthermore, a unique piece of their body was removed. Three of the four were killed by wounds to the main artery. That said, each of those implemented a different method. All would have died relatively quickly from blood loss. Explains why nobody in attendance heard anything."

An excited shiver ran through Aurélien's spine. He only hoped Inspector Holloway saw it as one of disgust. "What a horrific way to go. These parts that were missing, were they taken while they were alive?"

"Hard to say. That room was roaring like the engine of locomotive when we came to the scene. Sped up some things quite a bit."

"Gray wasn't able to tell what organs were taken. Care to fill in the gaps?"

Inspector Holloway flipped a few pages in his notebook. "You're keen to know a lot of sensitive details. If this gets out to the papers, it'll be your head."

Aurélien only smiled and waited for the man to continue.

"Nails. Kidney. Eye. Oesophagus. Wrist. Barbaric, if you ask me. Trophies. If I didn't know better, I'd say there's a mass murderer on the streets of London."

Aurélien feigned disgust. "A mass killer? Say it isn't so."

Inspector Holloway took a long look around the room. "Had a few gruesome killings over the years, but recently they've become more macabre. A duke met his end a few weeks back. Duke Isaac Cromwell. We ruled it as a debt collector making an example out of him, but a few of us in Scotland Yard are hardly convinced. Some have taken to calling him The Knightsbridge Sculptor."

"I remember. I had been at the gathering where he was killed. I left well before the commotion. I can supply my account again, if the Yard has lost my initial interview." Aurélien paused for a moment, studying Inspector Holloway with an inquisitive gaze. He couldn't quite parse this strange line of questioning. He was either the worst inspector within Scotland Yard or he was trying to pry damning information from him. "Why are you telling me this?"

"For the simple reason that I know you were at both crime scenes."

Aurélien raised an eyebrow. He knew there was no chance that this human had any evidence against him. Only a coincidence and the word of drunk nobles to go off of. "A simple coincidence."

"We'd like you to come down for questioning." Inspector Holloway smiled. It came off more like a grimace than anything else. "We can do this in the civil way or, if you'd prefer being in the broadsheets, the constables here can take you in with irons."

The last of his liquor went down in a single swallow. Talking his way out of this human made setback would take time.

Time he didn't necessarily have or wish to waste. Killing the men would only raise more suspicions—more than likely condemn him to the gallows, not that a demon was afraid of dying. Leaving his cells would make his human facade much more difficult. A life of hiding was not how he wished to spend his days once free from his owner.

"I will come without irons. Please allow me to go spin a tale for my guests. It will only take a moment."

✝✝✝

The room he was guided to was one of the nicer offices within Scotland Yard's headquarters. It spoke of his status. Had he been a commoner, he would have been tossed in a cell to stew for hours before being brought to a dingy room for questioning. Instead, Aurélien was offered tea by a secretary. It was cheap and bitter; no amount of sugar or milk was saving it—not that he was offered any in the first place.

He was left alone for quite some time, enough to gather the minute details of the office. It certainly wasn't Inspector Holloway's office. An engraved plate at the front of the desk read *Chief Inspector Henry Baker* in a similar font to the engravings on a cheap tombstone. He vaguely recognized the name—one of his father's old smoking friends, no doubt.

An hour after being brought in, the chimes of Saint Martin's bells rang as morning turned into afternoon. Not long after a man in a neat suit with a well-kept mustache entered the room trailing the scent of cigar smoke and fish from his lunch. He looked quite a bit older than he remembered but this was indeed the Henry Baker his father knew. "Ah, Lord Saint-Orlant, I am terribly sorry to have kept you waiting. My subordinates didn't inform me you were waiting in my office until I returned from lunch. Have you waited long?"

Aurélien plastered a smile on his face. "Not long at all."

The door behind him opened and closed. Inspector Holloway entered and stood beside Chief Inspector Baker while the older man settled into his seat.

Aurélien continued on with pleasantries. "How have you been faring?"

"Quite well. I saw your father recently, in fact."

"Really? I wasn't aware he was in the city." Aurélien knew well enough his father had been in the city, skulking about on his territory. Destroying his art. "Passing through on business, I'm sure. You know how he is."

"Chief Inspector—" Inspector Holloway began. He was cut off by a hand rising to silence him.

"Inspector Holloway, I expect a good reason as to why you've wasted the time of a good citizen like Saint-Orlant." The old man opened a drawer of his desk and pulled out a cigar box. Snipping the end of one, he offered it to Aurélien, who graciously accepted. Aurélien lit it with a match, drinking in the pungent smoke.

"I believe he thinks I'm a mass murderer—The Knightsbridge Sculptor," Aurélien supplied, grinning widely at Inspector Holloway when the old man turned his head.

"Preposterous! Where is your evidence?" Chief Inspector Baker fumed.

"Four murders occurred under his roof just yesterday. I believe the culprit also had a hand in the death of Duke Isaac

Cromwell some weeks ago. Saint-Orlant was in attendance during that event. That is five murders he has been in the vicinity for."

Aurélien hung his head mournfully. "As I explained, I left the gathering at the Cromwell's estate relatively early with my companion. I've been in attendance at a fair share of parties this social season."

"Do you have any *actual* evidence, Holloway?"

"Only his suspicious activities, sir." Inspector Holloway looked at Aurélien from the corner of his eye. "The murders last night differed from the Cromwell case—"

The old man muttered, "Oh, not this again."

"A series of parts were removed. Nails. Wrists. Kidney. Eye. Oesophagus. If you arrange the first letter of each word, and substitute eye for an I, it spells out: *I. K.N.O.W.*" Inspector Holloway set a report before the chief inspector. "These were all deliberate choices and odd choices for trophies."

"How does this connect Lord Saint-Orlant to being some—some mass murderer?"

"You didn't see the den of debauchery within his estate."

Aurélien couldn't help but laugh, he kept his head down in an attempt to hide his amusement. "Inspector Holloway, if my soirée was so stimulating for you, I worry for your wife."

"I don't have a wife," Inspector Holloway muttered.

"Pity. Perhaps devote yourself to the church then? Father Beausoliel has an exceptional sermon about the sins of the flesh. You simply must sit in on it when he returns from his sabbatical." Aurélien looked Inspector Holloway up and down, a knowing smile. He blew a cloud of thick smoke from his lips. An ashtray was slid over to him which he nodded his gratitude and tapped off the ashes from his cigar. "I can assure you; it was a fairly tame event despite what Inspector Holloway says. I'm simply following my father's request to find a wife. Father Beausoliel and my brother, Theodore, can attest to this."

Chief Inspector Baker stood, smoothing his clothing as he did so. "Scotland Yard appreciates your cooperation, Lord Saint-Orlant. You're free to go. I can see, clearly, that there is no reason for you to be here."

Aurélien snuffed out the end of his cigar. "My pleasure, Chief Inspector. I want to see this murderer caught as much as anyone else."

A few more pleasantries were exchanged before Aurélien turned on his heel to leave. He was glad to be out of this damned place. It set him on edge being scrutinized, even by someone like Inspector Holloway.

"Sodomy!" Inspector Holloway's voice rang out. It stopped Aurélien in his tracks.

Chief Inspector Baker scoffed. "You're accusing a good citizen of Her Majesty's England of such a blasphemous act? Consider your words before you speak them, Holloway."

Aurélien walked calmly back to the desk, keeping it between him and the two mortals. They didn't scare him. Nothing did as of late. Angered? Hated? Disdain? He felt each one. But fear? Fear slipped away from him the moment he became whole again. At that moment he felt only anger—burning rage at the audacity this pesky mortal had. Aurélien never trusted Inspector Holloway to keep his mouth shut. It really was only a matter of time before it slipped out, but he had at least hoped for enough time to end his contract before it happened. "Sodomy, hm? What proof do you have of this charge?"

Chief Inspector Baker nodded his head. "Yes, what evidence do you have for this?"

"My own eyes, Chief Inspector. I saw him—"

"Saw me in prayer?" Aurélien interjected, practically sneering. "Saw me in prayer with Father Beausoliel after a close friend perished under my own roof? You truly think me so—so disgusting that you would accuse me of *sodomy*?"

"I have countless witness testimonies."

"You never saw a single thing. Only what drug addled minds thought they saw. You would dare imprison me because of the hallucinations of the blue blooded?"

The old man's face had gone pale. "Well, this won't do. Tell me it isn't so, Lord Saint-Orlant."

"He fornicated with a priest," Inspector Holloway added.

Aurélien stared at him blankly. This was all so childish. The man was lashing out, throwing a tantrum because he didn't get his way. He was costing Aurélien his life outside of the underworld. How fucking annoying. Aurélien was growing tired of trying to talk his way out of the situation. Those witness reports would be an issue. "And if this is true, what will you do to me?"

"We'll throw you in prison to rot until the noose is ready." Inspector Holloway glowered at him; an ugly mug folded even more so by that scowl. "You're a disgrace. It goes against God to partake in such blasphemy."

A low laugh let itself out of Aurélien, growing louder and louder until he could only throw back his head and enjoy it. His sealing ring struggled to contain the beast within. As he spoke the anger ripped itself through his glamour bit by bit, exposing these men to what he truly was. "What the Hell has your God ever done for me? Did God intervene when I was created? Did he send his angels to pray over me while I split over and over into a demon? No, he didn't bloody help. But you know who did? Celio helped. My lilithspawn helped. He saved me when no fucking God could."

"Merciful Jesus!" Chief Inspector Baker threw himself back, knocking into the other mortal. His chair fell backwards, twisting up in his own legs causing both him and Inspector Holloway to fall to the floor.

Aurélien picked up the paperwork regarding his case—pathetically written in a sloppy hand. He leafed through it idly, enjoying the terrified breathing coming from the mortals in the room. Each witness statement was plucked out and burned between his fingers. He wasn't a monster, though, dropping the ashes onto the ashtray still holding the end of his cigar. When he was done, Aurélien smiled, baring sharp teeth. "I believe we have a new understanding, don't we? This case is dropped. The killer has gotten away. If I so much as hear a single word about this case again, I will drag your souls by your cocks to be punished in Hell."

He was met with silence and unblinking, wide eyes. "Nod!"

Quick nods happened. Aurélien could hear the vertebrae in one of their necks groan with how quickly they moved.

"W-What are you?" the useless old man asked.

Aurélien shrouded himself in his glamour again, rolling his shoulders as his wings slipped away. Darkness surrounded them, sealing them off from the humans of London, throbbing with the pulsing of his heart. Black twisted around and around creating a silent world. It surprised Aurélien but he kept a firm expression on his face. There was an innate feeling within that assured him the darkness would bend to his will. His blood listened to him—it was still a part of him. He desired silence and thus it was given. "I am the Dark Prince Aurélien, son of the Morning Star—and I will not take orders from fucking mortals any longer. Speak of this and you will not see the next sunrise."

A gunshot rang out. Black blood bubbled from Aurélien's throat, the faintest of pain burning through his flesh. He coughed—or tried to, blood rushing up to his mouth making his gag. Again and again, he coughed until the bullet came out and the wound healed. All the while he stared at Inspector Holloway and his smoking pistol. No wonder Axædus had laughed at his own attempt. He stepped forward and dropped the blood covered bullet onto Inspector Holloway's lap. "My turn."

The weapon he had received just hours before appeared in his hand, barely even a thought needed to conjure it. Inspector Holloway fired three more shots—all but one missed, a stray bullet clipped his shoulder. It barely even registered in his mind that it happened, the pain was as minimal as a needle prick. Aurélien raised his gun and fired a single round into the man's chest.

Unlike his brother, Inspector Holloway stayed down. He crumpled and fell, not even making a sound. The chief inspector, however, shook and gasped—it's a wonder how a man as pathetic as he was had made it so long in the field. "It's nothing personal, Baker. I've got my life on the line here. Should've kept a tighter leash on your men."

"I won't say anything! Please, let me live. I have a wife and children. I won't speak a word!" Sniveling. Groveling. It never worked on Aurélien. He was at least glad this one didn't start offering his children up like poker chips to gamble with.

"That's the thing about humans, Baker, they fucking *lie*." He pulled the trigger again, the darkness around them swallowing the sound. Aurélien brought the barrel up and breathed in the scent of gunpowder. It was a euphoric scent.

Reaching down, he plucked a clump of his congealing blood. "Tell Celio I require his assistance."

The blood gurgled in his hand then opened three eyes that stared up at him. It fussed more until chicken-like feet sprouted and stood up. The creature dashed about on his palm for a moment before jumping down and rushing off. It slipped through the window, squishing between the woodwork.

Aurélien spent a moment looking through the files strewn across the desk for any further incriminating evidence. What little he found he burned.

"You can make golems now. How cute," Celio said, in lieu of greeting. He appeared in a smoky haze not unlike how Axædus did. Celio whistled, looking over the bodies. "That bad, huh?"

"Tedious."

A small, inquisitive hum. "Humans are easy to fool, so we have that to our advantage."

Aurélien leaned against the desk and ran Celio through the plan. As much as he would love to be rid of his human life, there was use in having a good societal standing. Being seen leaving the crime scene was unlikely to end well.

Celio pouted. "You want me to turn into that ugly old man? He's not even close to being cute."

"Yes, you need to escort me out of the building then make your way back inside. Stop and chat with someone, mention you may have to demote Holloway, then come back to this office. We'll stage a fight; fire two rounds and we leave before the door can be opened." Aurélien sighed, briefly laying out a few quips and lines to possibly say in their faux fight.

"Simple enough," Celio murmured, turning himself into Chief Inspector Baker. "I want a reward for this, Little Love."

"And you'll get one when we get home, darling. No need to pout."

✝✝✝

Being released from custody was child's play. Such a thing would have been leagues easier had Aurélien not resorted to shooting two inspectors, but he was quite pleased to be escorted out of the halls of Scotland Yard. He smiled at constables as they walked past, keeping a cool demeanor until they were outside.

Aurélien watched Celio walk back inside then made himself scarce, swinging down the nearest alleyway to disappear without raising suspicion. He appeared back in the chief inspector's office a few moments later and waited out of sight patiently while guised as Holloway. When Celio entered, the fight began.

"You've just let the best lead we had in this case waltz free!" Aurélien bellowed, his voice a perfect match to the now deceased Inspector Holloway.

Celio locked the door behind himself. "Holloway, that good man has done nothing to be under such scrutiny."

"Scrutiny! He was at the scene of the crime!"

"As was half of the young upper class! Being present is hardly a motive." Despite their yelling, both demons smiled. It was quite exhilarating to fight with no real anger behind it.

"Chief Inspector Baker, I—"

"There's nothing more to say here. You've insulted a very powerful man's son today. We are terribly lucky I am such good friends with the Saint-Orlant family."

"Good police work is being ignored on account of friendship! You're corrupt!"

"Another word of this Holloway and I will demote you. Six months of desk duty ought to set you right!"

"Six months? Six months! People are being hunted and you've let the suspect go free." Aurélien picked the gun off of Inspector Holloway's corpse, aiming the weapon at the chief inspector's body that was cooling at their feet.

"I said not a word more and again you defy me. Holloway, I want you to go home, sleep whatever is bothering you off, and report to my office tomorrow morning for disciplinary action. This will not go unpunished." Celio plucked the gun out of the holster the dead chief inspector wore. He cocked the hammer back, ready for Aurélien's cue.

"Fine. If I have to go through you to get justice for those dead, then so be it."

"Holloway, put that gun down! We can talk about this like reasonable adults."

Aurélien nodded his head and they each fired a gun. Celio dropped his gun and they spirited themselves away before the door was successfully knocked down.

†Lust†

Theo slammed the morning broadsheet down in front of Aurélien during the morning meal several days after Aurélien's run in with the Yard. It hadn't even been pressed yet, still curled up from how Theo carried it inside.

"Was this you?" Theo asked, pointing at the headline. Sketches of the crime scene were plastered on the front page. There was less blood than Aurélien remembered, but he chalked it up to artistic liberties.

TWO INSPECTORS DEAD IN SCOTLAND YARD SHOOTING

Chief Inspector killed by demoted inspector's gunfire.
—says eyewitnesses

Aurélien shrugged. "Are you accusing me of something?"

"No, but—"

He folded up the newspaper, tucking it under his arm. Aurélien stood, ignoring the squawk from Theo's mouth. "But nothing. Ignore this drivel for it has nothing to do with me."

"I think it has a lot to do with you," Theo snipped. "You're not in this alone anymore."

"I was never *alone* in this. I just didn't have some human trying to get in my way."

Theo rolled his eyes. "God, as if I'm *some* human. Like it or not, we were raised together. Blood or no blood, we're brothers. I don't give a shit if you're some demon now, I can still tell you you're being an asshole. Tell me the truth, Aurélien."

Aurélien grit his teeth. His brother had always been agitating even under the best circumstances. "Fine. I killed them. Happy? It'd be a bloody mess if I hadn't."

The human thought for a moment, as if debating the validity of his claims. "Alright, I believe you. But you can't just keep killing humans as you please. Someone will catch on sooner or later."

"Mm." It wasn't an agreement, but an acknowledgment. He couldn't promise not to kill humans. If his master commanded it, he would have to see that the deed was done. Truthfully, the act never had to be bloody, but Aurélien had always been one for theatrics. Celio had claimed to adore his art, thus Aurélien kept creating it whenever he had the chance. His medium was gore, and his creations were drenched in it. When this contract was complete, he wondered if he would be able to create masterpieces for Celio in Hell. Aurélien wandered to the windows, looking out at the dreary day that had been dragged into London.

"When are we going to do it?" Theo asked, taking a seat at the table.

"Soon. Head back to his estate and once there, convince that disgusting beast to invite me home for a visit. Perhaps his rotten brain won't think twice about it. He knows I've done something to our contract and he's beyond angry about it."

"How do you know he's aware?"

"One of those pigs informed me they had met with him just this week. He knows all right—and what he did to my art, to my creations, proves it. It proves he's more than just some feeble old man with piss and shit for brains." Aurélien seethed just thinking about that man. He wanted nothing more than to tear his skull from his body and crush it beneath his feet. Aurélien hated him for what he did, for everything that he made him. Aurélien didn't hate the demon he was, far from it, but he mourned the human life he had come to adore. The simple routine of wandering the streets and spending his time within The Church of Sanctuary. Part of him missed the simplicity. He wished he could go back to when the most difficult thing in his existence was loving a priest.

"I'll leave tonight," Theo promised. "What then? Once you arrive home that is. I'm to kill our father. How do you want me to do it?"

"Wren has a lover in the trade business. Underground sort of shit. I'll ask him to procure the most lethal poison in China, Hell—the whole world."

"Poison seems rather… simple." Theo drummed his fingers against the table. Agitated and anxious to the point of losing his manners.

"Would you rather slit his fat throat yourself? Bone is harder to cut than you would expect."

"I'm not complaining, poison is perfectly acceptable to me. I just wonder if it's too simple for you. You'd much rather make a show of it, I can tell."

Aurélien laughed. "No lost love between you and that man then?"

"Heavens no. Father was always… he's been a monster to me even before—this," Theo said, voice uneven. "I've wanted him dead for a long while. Hard not to when he beats Mother like he does. I want her out of there, but she's so far under his control she doesn't even see how wrong it is."

Aurélien knew all too well the man's anger. He too had been struck by him more times that he could count, Theo as well, but neither mentioned it. Vivienne, Theo's mother, and the woman who raised Aurélien after his own mother's death, was far more important. "We'll see him dead, Theo, you have my word."

"And after? You're the heir. Will Mother and I... will you keep us safe? I can work now that I'm... fixed, but it will take me some time to learn the business. I wasn't raised into it like you were. God, how will I tell Mother about him? She's visiting Grandmother for the season. She can't find out through a telegram."

"*Fixed*? Theodore you're as man as you've always been. The outside just matches the inside now," Aurélien corrected, smiling. "Remember that for me and you can do whatever the Hell you want with the Saint-Orlant estate."

"What about you? What will you do when this is all over?"

Aurélien shrugged. He hadn't allowed himself to think that far. Not with so much at stake. This attempt could easily lead to his death. Nobody had said it, but the demons at his side—his Celio, they all knew and knew well enough not to speak it. "Might stay in London a while with Celio or maybe I'll go to Hell and meet my father. I've got a few choice words to say to him."

"You better treat your priest well. He's good... bad?" Theo paused, contemplating the phrasing. "He's good for you."

He Who Bleeds

✝✝✝

The Church of Sanctuary loomed before him, as inviting as any forgotten church of the Lord. A storm had rolled into London, heavy sheets dropping over the streets. Aurélien raced into the towering stone structure, Celio on his heels screaming his discontent for their circumstances.

It was dry inside, chilled regardless of the fires that burned in an attempt to warm the massive church. Aurélien allowed Hellfire to flash across his flesh, drying the damp so his shoes stopped squeaking as he walked.

"Wren? Are you here?" Celio called, stalking to the altar of the church. It was blissfully empty and the lilithspawn spent a moment lighting the hundreds of candles within.

Aurélien swallowed at the sight of Celio behind the altar, the incubus dressed in his old cassock again for the occasion. The sight was tantalizing, making his mouth practically water in anticipation. He had forgotten how delectable the view was. It should have been no surprise how easily Aurélien had strayed from God's path. For over ten years he had longed to have the Lord's loyal servant and now he had him. He finally had him to defile on the unholy altar.

Celio tore his gaze from the false Bible upon the stand, a knowing look in his eyes. Playfully he scolded, "Naughty."

"Forgive me, Father Celio for the late hour, but I desperately need to make a confession."

"Do not defile my confessional!" Wren scolded as he entered the room. He was shirtless, his trousers half unbuttoned.

The three sisters poked their heads out from the door he came from, watching.

"This is *my* church. I will defile it how I please," Celio scoffed.

"Why are you here?" Wren asked, raising a brow. The sisters gathered around him, all equally undressed as he was. Aurélien looked each one over. Beautiful—more prepossessing than any human could hope to be. Though, they would never be his Celio.

"I need you to procure a poison. Something strong. I want the bastard dead fast," Aurélien said, making his way to the leftover wine. He poured it into the silver chalice, filling it to the brim. It tasted cheap and bitter. "You would think the son of God would have better tasting blood."

"Poison is a weakling's tool," Wren remarked. He looked Aurélien up and down as if considering his own words. "Have you become weak?"

"It isn't for me. For Theo. He has agreed to slip it into his father's meal."

"A knife through the throat is easier. Faster, too," the false deacon lamented. He sighed, obviously displeased with the task he was given. "Give me a few days. Jiang is hard to track down on short notice."

Celio took the chalice from Aurélien's hands, sampling the wine. He drank down half, a drop trailing down his chin. "You're right, this wine does taste foul. Are you drinking the good wine, harlot?"

Wren smiled, not hiding his guilt. "Why waste it on humans when the sisters and I can enjoy it so much more?"

"I told him not to," Lavinia remarked, turning up her nose as if the mention of subpar wine was revolting.

"I'll come visit your townhouse when I've got the poison. Give me a week." Wren turned back towards the door, the sisters trailing after him.

The door had barely clicked closed when Aurélien guided Celio in for a kiss. Claiming with a little too much teeth. Aurélien's hands were on him, roaming his vestment draped body.

Celio moaned into the kiss, moving closer to him. His back was pressed against the altar, the large wooden piece shifting slightly with the force Aurélien used.

"I want to fuck you on this altar. Worship you. Create sin from our flesh. I wish to take His lost lamb and defile him. Will you let me?" Aurélien kissed along his throat, leaving his mark where he could. With two hands on his plump rear, Celio was lifted onto the table. The Bible fell with a loud thump, pages crushed under the weight of itself. Aurélien slipped his hand beneath Celio's vestments, sliding up to the incubus' thigh.

"Destroy me and recreate me in His true image. Make me *yours*." Celio pressed up, trying to move Aurélien's hand to his cock. He pushed up his cassock, undoing the clasps upon his trousers to free his pathetic cock.

"You speak so sweetly when you want something. You want this as much as I. How often did you think of this as you preached your sermons?" He nipped at Celio's flesh again.

"Often—too often. I wanted you to take me upon this altar before all to see." Celio gasped, a warm hand engulfing his cock. Aurélien stroked slowly, wringing out his desires. The pleasure twisting on the false priest's face was as fine as the most expensive wines. His chest rose and fell with quick, desperate breaths. His small erection was hard in Aurélien's grip. The devilspawn smiled, drinking in the sounds slipping from the other. He considered kneeling before him, taking his small cock into his mouth and tasting every inch of his length. As he considered the future pleasure he would draw from the man, the lilithspawn continued on, "I wanted to tear a hole in the wicker of the confessional and let you use my mouth for your divine worship."

No other words needed to be said. Celio was lifted and carried unceremoniously to the confessional booth. Aurélien opened one side and, with little care, dropped the false priest inside. The opposite side was soon occupied, only a thin wicker piece between them.

Aurélien looked upon the intricate weaving he once revered and, at the height of his cock, punched his fist through the material. He could see the shadows of Celio through the wicker, the incubus removing his clothing before he knelt before the newly created hole.

"Let me taste you." Celio used his fingers to rub away the rough broken pieces of wicker. He pressed close to the hole and opened his mouth.

"You're nothing but a whore," Aurélien spat, jamming two fingers into the waiting mouth. Celio didn't gag as he pressed down, letting the soft, pink tongue coat his fingers with saliva. A pleading, hungry little sound slipped from his incubus' gaping mouth. "You like this, don't you?"

A subtle nod of the head and, had it not been for the fingers in his mouth, Aurélien would have missed it.

"Oh, you do, don't you?" Aurélien teased, pressing down on his tongue. It licked up at his fingers, tasting—wanting. "Be a good little harlot for me, Celio."

His cock strained against his trousers, and it took considerable strength not to tear them off his body like a creature in heat. Aurélien freed his erection and pressed it through the hole into the waiting mouth of his hungry lilithspawn. Kitten licks greeted him, tasting every drop of precum from his cockhead. He thrust slowly, rolling into the delicious heat of the false priest's mouth.

Celio sucked and licked, letting his mouth hang open. He didn't choke or gag against the intrusion. His hands pressed against the wicker divider, crushing it between his fingers until they had something to hook into.

"That's it. Good whore." Aurélien fucked into his mouth, groaning at the sensation of pliant wetness. His whore whined around his cock, the sound of his desires filling the space between them. He thrusted with little care for the other's pleasure, chasing his own release with only release on his mind.

Celio was only a wet hole for him. There was no demon attached to the waiting mouth. He was but a vessel to usher in the devilspawn's pleasure. The old wood of the confessional booth groaned under the rocking motion of their bodies, threatening to crash down around them.

The torn wicker rubbed against his exposed skin occasionally, the pain giving way to pleasure with ease. He wanted more. Aurélien pulled away as his orgasm neared. It was too soon to end his destruction of God's home. He needed to spill his seed across the altar of the Lord and mark this false priest as Hell's property. As *his* property. This priest worshiped him. Not God. Not his dear father Lucifer, but *him*. Aurélien needed the world to know that this pathetic little incubus was his and his alone. No desecrated brother, depraved human master or any disgusting angels, should such beasts exist, would ever lay a hand on his priest—on his unholy person. Aurélien would anoint Celio with his seed upon the altar of the false Lord and all would know that the lilithspawn was his.

He tore Celio from the confessional booth, interrupting the pathetic pawing the incubus was doing to his own throbbing erection. Aurélien cared little for the false priest's pleasure, pulling him towards the altar. Celio stumbled behind him, whining his displeasure of having his orgasm cut short.

"You're going to offer yourself to me upon the altar." Aurélien pressed him against the altar, hands tracing the other's body. He gripped the front of Celio's vestments and tore a hole across his chest, exposing his hardened nipples to the chill air of The Church of Sanctuary.

"Little Love, claim me. Make an offering of me! I'm yours." Celio spread his legs, his cock tenting the skirt of his cassock.

Aurélien's resolve nearly snapped. He felt the pathetic, needy gaze of his prize make his erection twitch in anticipation. The devilspawn always got what he wanted, but not yet. Waiting made the prize all the more rewarding. Taking Celio's weeping cock in hand, Aurélien stroked him slowly—just enough to keep him at the brink of orgasm, but not enough to get there. "Don't cum. Don't you dare, not without my cock buried in you."

Rolling moans slipped from Celio, begging, and pleading for release Aurélien would not grant. "Fuck me—oh, please!"

His trousers were swiftly removed, exposing Celio's plump ass. Aurélien spit onto his hole before pressing two fingers deep into him. Celio threw his head back and choked out a scream, one mixed with equal parts pain and pleasure. "That's it. Scream for me. Say my name. Beg for my seed."

"Aurélien! Ah-hah—Aurélien!" Celio whined as Aurélien pumped his fingers in and out.

"Louder. Let the angels hear your worship of your true God!" As if to contradict his own demands, Aurélien kissed him deeply, pressing his tongue into the incubus' mouth. He drank in those sounds, tasting the Blood of Christ on Celio's tongue.

His fingers were removed, painted with blood that neither cared to acknowledge. Pain brought pleasure. It gave way to pure bliss neither the false priest nor the devilspawn could ignore. Aurélien thrust into his hole with one smooth thrust, unperturbed by their lack of lubrication. Blood would easily do and the pathetic lilithspawn begging for more under his cock was hardly complaining.

"So deep—so good—Aurélien, my love, my heart! Give me more!"

Aurélien obliged, fucking hard into him. The altar beneath them rocked and groaned under their weight. "That's it. Scream for me like a good whore."

He bit Celio's throat, drinking down the trickle of blood that graciously pooled onto his tongue. Aurélien moaned as he tasted, enjoying the sensations on his tongue almost as much as the tight, quivering muscle around his cock.

"F-For as the body… ah—Aurélien, oh—is one… hath many members…" Celio's prayer was silenced with another bite to his tender flesh.

Aurélien continued to thrust even as the altar began to splinter under their weight. He had little care for the house of the false Lord. As he buried his cock into the incubus, his way slicked with a mix of blood and precum, Aurélien came. He pumped his seed into the other like a beast in heat.

Arching his back up, Celio moaned his name in orison. Begging for salvation that would never come from a God who would never listen to a creature as foul as he.

Celio's stomach was painted with his own cum, smeared about due to Aurélien's uncaring fucking. He hummed, satiated and full. "This would have only been better if a man had been crucified before us."

"You are perverse." The devilspawn barked a laugh. "I like it."

✝ Homecoming ✝

The Saint-Orlant manor came into view after far too long stuffed into a carriage. It had been many years since Aurélien made the trek from London to Wolverhampton, and the several days' journey was less than pleasant. Aurélien desperately wanted to stretch his legs without bumping into the knees of Celio.

"We should have flown," Celio whined, pouting as he watched the estate come into view.

"As much as I wish it was so, soaring through the skies for hours would draw the wrong kind of attention. We're here to kill my owner. The less mortal suspicion upon the Saint-Orlant home the better."

Celio turned Aurélien's head, capturing his lips slowly—taking small sips of energy. "You are right, Little Love. As much as I wish to burn this place until only stones remain for what he has done to you, I shall listen to your orders."

"That's a good boy," Aurélien praised, kissing him again. His little lilithspawn would need all the energy he could get.

The carriage stopped before the front staircase and Bram, in all his swiftness, set out steps and opened the door for them.

"Return to London, Bram. We'll be here for some time."

"Very good, sir." Bram made relatively quick work on unloading their small set of luggage, one of which contained the carefully wrapped vial of poison procured by Wren for their cause.

As the stairs were ascended, the front doors swung inwards revealing an old butler. "We have been expecting you, Master Aurélien."

"Is Father around?" Aurélien asked in lieu of greeting the old man.

"Master Saint-Orlant is within his office at present. He will be available to you. Shall I show your guest to his room?"

Celio, who had been looking about the large foyer with curiosity, smiled. He had worn his vestments on their excursion, hoping to grant them a bit of luck from any mortal authorities. No God-fearing mortal would arrest a priest. "That would be most appreciated. I could do with a little freshening up before dinner."

"This way then, Father."

Celio walked behind the butler, eyes exploring the well-decorated rooms and halls they passed.

Eventually he parted ways, turning down a long corridor that seemed to get colder with every step. At the end of the hallway, Aurélien stopped before a massive wooden door that seemed larger than all the others despite it being identical to them. Just behind this door was his master, the man who masqueraded as his father for decades. Aurélien wanted nothing more than to strangle him with his own necktie and watch the light drain from his eyes. Or, perhaps, a knife through the heart, which he would then retract and reinsert until his master's flesh was comprised of only minced meat. He had dreamed of this for years when given the spare moment to keep his mind about him—thinking of ending the life of a shadow-cloaked mortal. Now, however, there was a face to these fantasies. A face he would tear from his corpse before the blood within cooled.

He Who Bleeds

Knocking was a kindness he would not afford Baron Montague Edwin Saint-Orlant. Aurélien opened the door with a slow, practiced turn of the knob so it didn't even click—an old habit from his childhood that, even now, he couldn't shake. He didn't care if he bothered the man once known as his father.

Montague sat at his desk with several ship's ledgers stacked before him. He didn't look up from his work, giving Aurélien ample opportunity to study his hideous disposition. Aurélien found the sagging of his jowls and the fine wisps of white hair still clinging to his head to be particularly revolting. Aging had never bothered Aurélien, and it never would. If he had to look upon such a horrid face each morning as a mortal, he would toss himself from the highest mountain peak—or perhaps a noose upon a sturdy beam. Whichever suited his fancy at the moment.

The room was sweltering, a fire burning despite the rather warm weather.

"Father." Aurélien sat in a chair across from the desk. He didn't pepper his words with false kindness. It wasn't due.

"Aurélien," Montague said, glancing up from the ledgers at last. "What do we owe the pleasure to?"

"Theo suggested I return home for a visit."

A low, unimpressed hum. "I hope you have followed my *suggestion* on finding a wife before returning to my doorstep."

"A wife. Something of the sort."

"Aurélien. A wife. A *good* wife of decent standing. Not a street whore who bears your seed." Montague sighed, scratching something into the ledger before him. "I need you to take this seriously. You need to start your family, and I am not getting any younger. For whom will I leave my empire upon my passing? Theodore has never expressed interest in it."

Dorian Valentine

Aurélien rolled his eyes. *Empire.* An ego riddled word for the pathetic merchant business Montague had built. Montague was a cockalorum in every sense of the word and the devilspawn longed to spit the word into his face. "I cannot recall ever desiring your *empire.*"

"I see you still have no head for logic. I thought after Vincent's untimely death, you would step up as the eldest son. Are you still enthralled with that barbaric excuse for a church? We are a good *Christian* family, yet you turn to Catholicism out of some perverse need. Your mother would be beside herself if she knew how far you strayed. You need to prioritize this family, our empire, before any spiritual journey you wish to embark on. If Vincent was still with us, I would have no qualms with a clergyman as a son, but Vincent has long since left this world. As it stands, you must be prepared to make sacrifices for the good of the Saint-Orlant family."

"Father Celio and I have developed quite a relationship since we last spoke, Father. He has guided me in ways you cannot imagine. Mortal faith has little to do with our rapport—and having a companion so high within the church is never a poor choice."

"It is a poor choice when it is a pollutant to your reputation! Do you know what the upper echelon says about that place? That it is a corrupt, devil-worshiping whorehouse with less pious aspirations than a fishmonger's stall." Montague scoffed, waving a hand to push away the disgusting airs that speaking about The Church of Sanctuary may have brought about.

Aurélien had to fight the urge to kill Montague right then and there. It would only end with a living human and a dead spawn. Had the contract not contained Section 27, Clause E, turning the man into minced meat would be as ancient as the Fall of Lucifer.

"You speak boldly for a man who has not seen the inside of a church since Theo's baptism. We both know religion has never been this family's priority."

"In the eyes of society, it is." Montague stood, turning his back to Aurélien, gazing out of the window at his sprawling estate. "I will arrange for you to meet the Bradshaw girl before you leave. She'll be good for you. Just turned eighteen. The Bradshaws are a good family. Joining with them will be prosperous for us all."

"I have no intentions of marrying." Aurélien scowled, barely holding back an annoyed, animalistic growl. This conversation was dull and far from worth his time. Montague would be dead within hours and there would be no wife in his future. What use did he have for a wife when he kept neither house nor home? Needless to say, he had no intentions of continuing on his infernal lineage, he had enough siblings writhing in Hell to make up for the loss of one broodmare. Regardless, Aurélien had Celio, and his incubus was jealous like no other. Bringing the wrath of a demon with God's exorcism rights memorized upon himself would be, to put it simply, less than ideal.

"Son, you are over thirty now. We must all do things we dislike for the sake of family. Did you think I married your mother for love? Far from it. I was fifteen years her senior. She and I came to care for one another, so too will you and the Bradshaw girl." The man previously called father glanced over his shoulder at Aurélien. If he had the opportunity, Aurélien would stab the letter opener which laid on the desk before him into the back of that wretched man. He would stab until the flesh grew cold and the blood ceased leaking from the corpse.

Without giving a response, Aurélien stood. He couldn't be in the room with him any longer. It always ended like this, even when he thought he was wholly mortal. In some charged, tense words that ended when one relented or a glass broke against the wall. "I shall see how Father Celio is settling in."

Montague turned around quickly, his voice barely holding back his anger. "You brought that miscreant into my house?"

"I will see you at dinner, Father."

✝✝✝

The false priest had sprawled across Aurélien's bed, the various chests rummaged through and tossed about with little care for order. Aurélien paid it no mind, stepping over clothes so he could lay upon the bed with his lilithspawn.

"I'm going to kill that man if it's the last thing I do."

Celio rolled onto his stomach, propping his head up in his clawed hands. "We both want to, Little Love. That man is… is, well I don't have the words to describe that bastard. Let us rest easy knowing his soul will burn in Hell's deepest fires before the sun rises again."

"What happens once this is all over?" There still existed the faintest sliver of humanity within Aurélien, one that reared its head at Celio's promise. He still felt the deep human fears that had yet to be consumed by his demonic blood. Within was still the boy who prayed in The Church of Sanctuary, the man in love with a priest—the human afraid of a God who never answered his prayers. A man with doubts and reservations that needed answers not even his demonic self could provide.

"We go to Hell. Wren and the sisters will be released from their duties and the fires of Hell will reach up and take us down into the inferno below." Celio smiled, reassuring. Aurélien wondered if the incubus ever felt consumed with the human facade he oft wore. If those lies ever twisted into truth. "I expect you'll appear before The Dark Lord's throne. His Infernal Majesty will bless you with the true strength of your powers. Perhaps He will even grant you rewards if He sees fit. And if He is magnanimous, He may allow me to remain in your service."

Aurélien reached up, tucking a piece of hair behind Celio's pointed ear. "You are an adequate hole to fuck. I'll keep you around for a while yet. Another century perhaps."

"The incubi trained by Az are quite skilled. You will enjoy them, but not nearly as long as you will me. They break easily, dainty like dolls of bone China. Disposable. Keep me. I know you. I know every inch of you and every way to bring you pleasure." Celio grabbed his hand, placing a kiss at the pulse of Aurélien's wrist. He looked at him with lust filled eyes, biting into the flesh with his sharp fangs.

Pleasure ran through Aurélien's body, each nerve shivering with the pure potency of the false priest's lust. Celio moaned ever so quietly as he drank a mouthful of blood before Aurélien withdrew his hand. "We have a mission at hand, Celio. As much as I wish to ravish you at this moment, our desires must wait until the human is dead."

"An unholy coupling drenched in his blood awaits us, Little Love."

Without so much as the kindness of a knock, the door to the bedroom was open then promptly shut behind Theo. He looked around warily at the disarray within the room before spying the demons lounging upon the goose down bed. "You've made it. Do you have the… do you have it?"

"You've destroyed our luggage, priest, where is it?" Aurélien asked, pushing the clingy demon away so he could stand.

Celio listened to the request, meandering to an ornate wooden box nestled within one of the many chests. He handed it over to Theo, barely holding back a yawn as he explained the brew within. "Wren said just a few drops will do the trick. Empty the whole bottle, if you want to be thorough—but the bastard may taste it."

Hands that had never seen a day of work in their life opened the box as though removing betrothal gifts. The vial was removed from the padding of silks inside, a pale liquid sloshing about inside. "This is it? It seems… less than I expected."

"What did you expect?" Celio dropped the now purposeless box onto the floor.

"I cannot say what I expected. More, perhaps. This liquid is enough to rend a man of his life? Why, it looks like puddle water." Theo sighed and pocketed the vial. "I'll add this to the coffee. I suggest avoiding such delicacies this evening."

There were still small gifts existing in the cursed world, yet Aurélien found himself doubting the plan in the final hour. The inevitable death of the man who held his life in his knobby hands was before him. A death that would come about with the slip of a hand and a tear's worth of poison. So easy. So *boring*—and completely out of his control. All this planning, all the artless death because of a contract signed on his behalf before conception. Nothing angered Aurélien more than the inability to act for himself.

Finally, after years of pointless slavery, Aurélien would be free.

†Patricide†

Patience was not a trait the devilspawn ever learned. Feigning interest was something he struggled with as well. As Aurélien listened to the dull chatter over dinner, he wished the poison had been placed into the first course. Discussions of weather, politics, and, because of Father Celio's presence at the dinner, religion's place in society, were unimportant, dull topics that piqued neither interest nor curiosity.

Aurélien's only entertainment was watching Theo squirm the closer they came to sharing coffee in death. Each time a servant entered to refill wine or bring about the next course, Theo would tense, his eyes wide in a mix of fear and anticipation that Aurélien could almost taste. Fear had a musky aroma that he, as the demon on many men's shoulders, was well acquainted with. He could only compare it to an ill kept wine, old and thick with silt—yet still carrying the delicious aroma a drunk could never deny.

As he ate his meal of roasted fowl, all Aurélien could taste was the rolling fear that penetrated the atmosphere of the room. Coffee and tea was served in fine China edged with painted silver bands—which were terribly crafted as the banding rubbed away with every sip of tea. The plates and silverware had been the same, cheap faux copies of more beautiful works.

All aside from Montague opted to savor the freshly imported tea blend that a fellow merchant family gifted the Saint-Orlants. It tasted bitter even with a spoonful of sugar, tingling in

Aurélien's mouth like nettle stings. He chose to ignore it in favor of watching the disgusting master before him perish in agony.

Montague drank his coffee in measured sips, glancing between his presumably human children. "My sons, might I make a suggestion?"

"Of course, Father. It is imperative that we listen to your advice." Aurélien smiled. He could feel Celio's hand on his thigh, tapping rapidly to gain his attention.

"If you attempt to poison a man, I suggest not defiling one of his few pleasures in life. Any subtle changes in taste becomes exceptionally apparent." The last dregs of poisoned coffee were drunk down, the cup set so gently upon its saucer it made not a single noise. "Might I suggest, as well, that you ensure your target has not been building a tolerance to such things for several decades."

Aurélien felt his upper lip twitch in barely veiled anger, held at bay only by the thin membrane of his sound mind. With a wide, toothy grin he asked, "Can you blame a demon for trying?"

"My son, you have been so very naughty. Have I not given you the world? All I ask is a little… assistance with regulating the competition from time to time. This breach of contract cannot be overlooked." Montague was not in a hurry when spoke. He possessed neither the rapid breath, shallow breath nor the panic of a rapidly dying man—but the slow drawl of an irate man. "I had been willing to overlook the interference of the weak demons surrounding you, Aurélien. Though you may be aware of your demonic heritage, it truly changed little in terms of our contract."

"You've had control of him for long enough, human." Celio gripped a dinner knife tightly in his hand, though made no move to use it.

He Who Bleeds

"How generous of you," Aurélien spat. He picked up his cup and made to throw it, but a burning pain shot up his arm in warning until he dropped it. Barely stifling a pained growl, he continued. "Soon you'll die, and I will spend eternity torturing your soul in Hell."

"Such are the terms of our contact. However, I have years yet and you are in need of punishment. Do forgive me for my Latin, it has been years." Montague retrieved a folded paper from within his jacket and cleared his throat. "Deus, cui próprium est miseréri semper et párcere: súscipe deprecatiónem nostram; ut hunc fámulum tuum, quem delictórum caténa constríngit, miserátio tuæ pietátis cleménter absólvat."

The words crept around his body, slithering against his limbs like chains—binding him. Every curve of a word burned into his flesh. Agony ran throughout his body as he felt his spirit rend from his flesh. The word of the false Lord burned his infernal soul.

Celio screamed in agony, the Latin prayer burning him as well. He was not nearly as strong as Aurélien, panting as he forced himself to stand, baring the dinner knife in a shaking hand.

Aurélien grit his teeth, unable to do anything to stop the words flowing from the old man. He summoned his pistol but no matter how hard he tried, he was unable to pull the trigger. Cursing under his breath, Aurélien swallowed the knowledge that they had been bested. The silver that flecked from their dinnerware buzzed under his skin in a godly reaction to Montague's prayers.

The wretched human continued his words, undeterred when faced with the seething rage of two demons. "Domine sancte, Pater omnípotens, ætérne Deus, Pater Dómini nostri Jesu Christi, qui illum réfugam tyránnum et apóstatam gehénnae ígnibus deputásti, quique Unigénitum tuum in hunc mundum misísti, ut illum rugiéntem contéret: velóciter atténdem accélera, ut erípias hóminem ad imáginem et similitúdinem tuam creátum, a ruína et dæmónio meridiáno. Da, Dómine, terrórem tuum super béstiam, quæ extérminat vineam tuam. Da fidúciam servis tuis contra nequíssimum dracónem pugnáre fortíssime, ne contémnat sperántes in te, et ne dicat, sicut in Pharaóne, qui jam dixit: Deum non novi, nec Israël dimítto. Urgeat illum déxtera tua potens discédere a fámulo tuo, ne diútius præsúmat captívum tenére, quem tu ad imáginem tuam fácere dignátus es, et in Fílio tuo redemísti: Qui tecum vivit et regnat in unitáte Spíritus Sancti Deus, per ómnia sæcula sæculórum. Amen."

"Father, stop! You're hurting them," Theo pleaded.

"Praepio tibi, quicúmque es, spíritus immúnde, et ómnibus sóciis tuis hunc Dei fámulum obsidéntibus: ut per mystéria incarnatiónis, passiónis, resurrectiónis et ascensiónis Dómini nostri Jesu Christi, per missiónem Spíritus Sancti, et per advéntum ejúsdem Dómini nostri ad judicium, dicas mihi nomen tuum, die et horam éxitus tui, cum áliquo signo: et ut mihi Dei minístro licet indígno, prorsus in ómnibus obédias: neque hanc creatúram Dei, vel circunstántes, aut eórum bona ullo modo offéndas."

With little grandeur, Aurélien's vision faded away into pitch darkness.

†Altar of the Morning Star

This was not death, Aurélien was sure of that much. If demons could truly die, he was unaware, but the fear of such a thing hardly deigned to cross his mind. Death would not come so easily for the son of the Morning Star.

He was no longer in the dining room. Even without opening his eyes to greet the darkness, he could tell he had been moved by the cold slab of stone beneath him. There was pain, of course, even a devilspawn felt pain—and what brought the pain was the crudely made stigmata on his body. He could feel the pulse of his flesh around the silver railroad spikes that held him in place—through his palms and each foot like a perverse son of God. Around each limb thin silver chains twisted across his bare body, marring his flesh with burns and sores.

"Little Love?" A familiar voice croaked from somewhere within the room. "Are you awake yet?"

"Mhm." Aurélien opened his eyes and was met with near darkness. Though the room was lit by dozens—possibly hundreds—of candles it remained shadowed. An unearthly darkness peered inside, watching their plight. Aurélien stared at the wooden beams above him, breathing through the pain. There was no stopping the agony, chained by silver—weakening him with each passing moment. They were pigs waiting for a slaughter that may never come. A false messiah to pair with the false priest caged above.

"Montague had better count his days. Locking me in this cage with these blessed chains. When I get out of here I—" Celio shifted, his own chains rattling. He sighed. Aurélien knew he was pouting just from the sound of it. "Are you faring better than I?"

"Chains. An altar. That bastard has me crucified. I've been made a martyr, I fear." Aurélien grit each word through the feeling of a crushing stone on his chest.

"Call for Ax."

"Celio—"

"Please. Whatever your owner is planning cannot be good. Using the divine word—silver—all of this? It speaks of ill tidings. Call Ax. Take his deal."

"And kill my favorite whore? Not likely."

Celio stifled a laugh. "Romantic."

The darkness crept closer, twisting around the stone altar Aurélien was an unwilling decoration upon. It formed, with no great effort, the shape of a man. Axædus stood over Aurélien with a wide smile. "Pitiful. Even now you value a tool so deeply you'd be willing to die for him. You lack self-preservation, dear brother."

"I do not need your help. Go to Hell." Demons did not love—a trait they were wholly incapable of, but they could be possessive. So much that it was a consuming adoration no mere human could possess. Loyalty and ownership were as close to love as a devilspawn could feel and feel it he did. Celio was his. The false priest was his to own and destroy and be worshiped by. No brother of chaos could force him to share his lilithspawn. Celio was his alone.

Axædus laughed, forcing Aurélien's head to turn to face him. "I intend to when this is all over. For now, however, I think

I'll watch your fall from grace—all because you want to keep your whore. Pathetic."

"Little Love… just let him—"

Aurélien tugged against his bindings, groaning as they dug into his flesh further. His tail flicked angrily against the altar. "There's one thing I hate in this life, and it's being told what to do. I'll always do the opposite. Thus I'll say again. Go. To. Hell."

"Say my name when you come to your senses, brother. Until then, I'll be enjoying this comedy from the shadows." Axædus turned to the cage Celio was contained in, which hung from the ceiling like a lark's cage. He reached up, and despite the singeing of his own flesh, spun the silver cage around and around. When he finished, laughing to himself, Axædus melted back into the shadows.

Aurélien didn't receive the luxury of even cursing his frustrations before there was movement outside their prison. Even muffled, he recognized Theo's voice, begging. "Father, you don't have to do this. Aurélien is—he'll—why don't we forget all of this?"

Rotting as he lived, the owner of his contract replied in haste. Montague's voice echoed throughout the hallway, muffled beyond stone walls, nearly hidden by the sound of dozens of footsteps. "You will do well to hold your tongue. I have forgiven your transgression; I can see your brother steered you in the wrong direction."

"Your father is right, Saint-Orlant. Keep out of our way." Another voice, one Aurélien did not recognize.

The sound of metal grinding filled the room. Aurélien hissed as the sound shot through his skull like a church's bell—ringing its foul melody. Several men entered the small room, singing their praise to Montague. The door closed once more, locking Theo from the chamber. No matter how hard he banged against the door, it would not open.

"Truly a feat no other has ever accomplished," a woman praised, sweeping into the room in a blur of Paris green that spoke of wealth and greed. She traced his cheek with the back of her hand and Aurélien growled as he attempted to bite her supple flesh for daring to touch what was not hers. From above, Celio hissed—reaching his arm out from between the bars of his bird cage.

Several more humans circled around the altar, watching Aurélien like the caged animal he truly was. They each wore masks of porcelain on their faces—he could smell the rot on them. All old and worthless, afraid of their own aging.

"Have you learned your place, child?" Montague asked, standing at Aurélien's head.

"I have been forsaken by God before I was even birthed from my mother's womb. I was created for a purpose—for you and your greed. That's what I am, aren't I? Your greed. Your demon. You've turned me into this, into a monster. You will feel my wrath until the end of your days! When Hellfire rains down on you, I will laugh." Aurélien thrashed against the silver chains, his bound wings writhing against them as he tried to pry himself free from the holy metal. "I will die before I bow to you ever again. Foul bastard. I will skin you whilst you live and use your flesh to wipe my cum off my whores!"

Montague chuckled to himself but otherwise ignored Aurélien.

"Will this work? Truly?" a man asked, drumming his fingers against the altar. "Will we be blessed with our youth once more?"

He Who Bleeds

"You will find that we have a perfect bargaining chip with the Dark Lord here. His son. If he would go to such lengths to conceive him, he will do this to have Aurélien returned to him." His owner held out a hand, a dagger being placed in it.

"I won't let you hurt him! Remove thine hands from my prince!" Celio screeched, reaching with all his might for Aurélien. He had no weapon, no powers to speak of—like Aurélien, Celio was trapped. Like Aurélien, he would die by the hands of greedy mortals.

"Enough of this. Let us begin. I can feel myself withering as we speak!" A woman wailed, cupping her face around the mask—the painted face grinned down at Aurélien, mocking him like a court jester.

"Patience," Montague chastised. He raised his knife and began etching a design into Aurélien's chest. Several hands, wrinkled and rubbery, held him down as his flesh was torn apart. He writhed, flexing wings and muscles to try and slip from under the knife, but the chains held him in place. The blade curled around his chest, blood pooling out under the sharp edge. Aurélien dared not look at the defilement of his body.

"Little Love… please, call for Ax," Celio begged. "Ax! Ax, I know you're here. Save him. I'll accept the deal."

The pleas were met with silence, followed by a cane hitting the silver cage. "Quiet."

"Should we wait until the full moon?" a man asked. He placed a hand on Aurélien's ankle, tracing up. The demon's skin crawled at his touch.

"The Dark Lord is no occult worship. We do not require the moon to summon His excellency. Only a worthy offering." A sigh—a pathetic sound from the man dressed in a black robe. Two of the women produced bronze bowls of herbs, striking matches to ignite the finely ground leaves. The scent mixed deliciously with the iron smell of blood. Aurélien's pupils blew wide as the strong redolence hit his nostrils, acting like catnip to street cats. The now high the devil's scion thrashed against his binds, screaming his anger—cursing every false god that would listen.

"O' Morning Star! O' Lucifer! Dark Lord, hear our prayers. We, thy loyal servants, offer to His Majesty a gift most foul. Thine son returns with our blades!" Montague raised his blade. "Come forth, Morning Star!"

The knife came down quickly. Aurélien tensed, preparing to feel the pain of his heart being pierced. Celio screeched, shaking the silver bars of his cage. It was nearly drowned out by the chanting prayers of the humans surrounding Aurélien.

The point of the knife stopped as it made contact with Aurélien's flesh, red beading out from beneath the wound to join the river that flowed. Aurélien turned his gaze towards the weapon, finding Montague struggling to press down further. Dark whispers of shadows twisted around the human's hands.

"My son, my Aurélien." A voice echoed through the chamber, deep and unnerving. "What a mess they have made of you."

"He's here! Praise!"

"Lucifer! Dark Lord, grant our prayers!"

"May He rise!"

A chorus of praises resounded, each human falling to their knees aside Montague, who was forced to remain in place by the shadowed hand.

"Dark Lord, grace us with your presence!"

He Who Bleeds

"F… Father? Dark Lord…?" Aurélien called, his breath shuttering under the growing presence of the Dark Lord before him. The Dark Lord—his true father. At last, He was before him, within grasp.

"Yes, my son. How you have grown. In quite a bind, I see." A laugh echoing around the chamber. The knife in Montague's grip melted away, turning to dust that pooled onto Aurélien's chest.

"You are observant, Father."

"Silence! You are mine to do with as I please until He accepts our terms." Montague yelled, tossing the wooden handle aside. "Dark Lord, if I may—"

A smoke covered hand slapped itself over Montague's wrinkled mouth. The Dark Lord hushed him with a soft sound like one would a crying child. From the soot dusted hand sprouted a mortal form—one beautiful beyond mortal compare. The Dark Lord looked like His sons, though untainted by the blood of mortal women. Aurélien dared to think Lucifer angelic in that moment, blond haired, warm tan skin, though what were once sapphire blue eyes had long turned red. Tainted by Hellfire and anguish. The Dark Lord was inhumanly tall, towering over all those in the room. He trained His red eyes onto Aurélien and smiled, showing off His sharp teeth. "Shh… This is not a time for mortals to speak, Saint-Orlant. I am here for my son."

Montague pulled out from the Dark Lord's grip, rubbing his mouth clean with the back of his sleeve. Aurélien found joy in the disgusted, off-put expression on his owner's jowl-riddled face. "Your *spawn* and his blasphemous priest have attempted to break the contract. I demand it be rectified with a new condition as penance."

"Spawn. What a cruel word. Are angels the spawn of God? He is my creation. My son. My pride. There is no need for cruelty." The Dark Lord swept around the altar as if floating, sending the humans scurrying about in fear like mice to a hawk's gaze. With His back to Aurélien, he could make out the disfigured, marred flesh along the Dark Lord's back—two perfect lines along His shoulder blades where wings had once sprouted, torn horrifically before His fall. Tilting His head with His inquiry, the fallen angel asked, "What is it that you desire, mortal?"

"Immortality!" A man brazenly cried, falling to his knees before the Dark Lord.

The Dark Lord's lips parted in an *O* shape. "My, how bold. Requesting such gifts with nothing to offer."

His hand shot forward, gripping the throat of the daring man. With no issue, the Dark Lord lifted the man from the floor—all while smiling. "You have no sway here, mortal. None of you do. Begone."

The shadows crept from the Dark Lord's hands, wrapping around the man's face, crawling across his body until he joined the darkness. There were no screams from the man's mouth as he was devoured by the night, nor did any escape from the various humans who waited with bated breaths for their due. The quivering excitement dissipated from the room as the cultists were erased from the realm of the living.

"You are a very brave human to summon me twice in your short life. Brave, but witless. Tell me, what is it that you desire?" the fallen angel asked Montague, sitting on the edge of the altar. He looked down at Aurélien. Hooking a finger beneath the silver chains, He plucked them like harp strings—each snapping under the touch. "How uncomfortable. Has Axædus been helping you? He has not been doing his duty well if this is his version of helping."

The railroad spikes did not burn in the Dark Lord's hand as they did Aurélien's, the holy metal nothing but common iron to Him. With his limbs free, Aurélien sat himself up on the altar, staring down the human who chained him to humanity for decades. "You bastard—"

"Saint-Orlant, I ask again, what is it that you dare desire?"

Montague swallowed, backing up several paces from the demons. "Immortality. I wish to live forever."

A wide grin slowly spread over His face. He turned His head to look at Montague. It turned naught like a human's, but twisted like an owl's, neck extending to allow for such movement—filling even His son with an uneasy feeling in the pit of his stomach. "Immortality. What makes you so worthy?"

"I still have work to do still within this world. An empire to run. Rivals to overpower. It must—" Montague's bleating was silenced by the Dark Lord's hand again.

"You must do *nothing*, human. What you must do is live a short pathetic life and die a wrinkled husk." The hand was withdrawn and rubbed dry on the black doric chiton He wore. "Your contact has been voided under Section 27, Clause F. No harm was to come to the contractor or else the contract is voided. My son has come under tremendous harm by your hand."

"He has tried to poison me!"

"Therein lies your confusion, mortal. My son did not commit the act, rather *your* son did." The Dark Lord chuckled. "You, however, raised a hand unto my child. Contract null and void."

Aurélien used the opportunity to release Celio from his cage, the skin on his fingers singing further as he touched the silver. Celio dropped down into Aurélien's arms, holding him tight. He ignored the squawking from Montague, focused on the burrowing grasp Celio had on him.

The false priest shook in his hold, tearing his way through Aurélien's name regardless of the pain it caused. "Au-rél—ien, A-Aur-élien, Aur—élien…"

Hunger rushed through Aurélien, flooding his senses with the scent of his flesh. He salivated, barely containing himself—the growl of a starving beast rolled from his throat.

Celio guided his head towards his neck, tilting to the side. "Taste of me. I will let you have a bite, Little Love."

The devilspawn had no disagreements with the offering, taking what was freely given with all the grace he could muster. Aurélien's fangs sunk into the meat of Celio's bare shoulder. The false priest cried out, stifling it behind the palm of his hand. Blood flowed from the wound as he bit away flesh. His incubus' flesh was like sweetmeat and Aurélien could see himself becoming more addicted to him than he already was.

A cold hand was placed on Aurélien's shoulder, guiding him away from the false priest's flesh with more strength than a gentle touch should have. The Dark Lord's voice was as gentle as His touch, sweet as He comforted His son. "You must be hungry, my son. Feasting on our Celio will not absolve that hunger."

Aurélien was tilted backwards into His arms. Lips met his, followed by the push of a forked tongue. The Dark Lord licked away the taste of Celio's flesh from inside of his mouth. Power flowed through the contact, his wounds stitching together with a buzz not dissimilar to the air before a storm. His tail shook with excitement and he, the son of the first fallen angel—God's favorite child, enjoyed every slow lick. The Dark Lord's hand wrapped around the base of Aurélien's tail, stroking the sensitive spot, forcing low purrs from the spawn.

The kiss deepened, the Dark Lord allowed His son to devour the power he required to live, their eyes remaining open— one set trained on the panting lilithspawn, the other on the frigid mortal who dared summon Him.

"Good boy," the fallen angel praised as Aurélien collected himself. Aurélien was gathered into Celio's arms who kissed away the taste of the Morning Star from his lips. The Dark Lord captured Celio's lips in one small kiss as He brushed by, the gifted power more than enough for the eaten flesh to return without scarring.

"Do not ignore me to fondle your child! Goddamned sodomites."

"Do not bring God into this. There is no God in these halls, only I." The Dark Lord sat upon the altar, even sitting, His statuesque form still towered over Montague. "Regardless, any claim to God's divinity you possessed, which was hardly worth mentioning, was forfeit the moment you made a deal with His least favorite angel. You are quite honestly nothing but a stain in God's eyes. A stain He would be pleased to see wiped clean from Terra."

"Our deal, Morning Star. You can be incestuous once we have completed our deal."

The Dark Lord tossed His head back and laughed, golden tresses slipping off His shoulders. "You have no say here, Saint-Orlant. Aurélien is no longer your slave. My son is free and you— you, you strange little creature, have nothing to offer me."

"I'm free?" Aurélien said softly, the words passing strangely over his lips. After years of wearing a leash held by a mortal, he was finally free.

The false priest kissed every inch of his face, smiling wide. "You are, my Dark Prince. We're free. We can finally return home. No more… God and prayer."

Montague raised his voice again, tearing Aurélien's attention away from Celio's wandering hands. "You have consumed several members of your cult, Dark Lord, all of which I have brought before you. These offerings surely are enough to grant I, Baron Montague Edwin Saint-Orlant, immortality."

The smile fell from the fallen angel's face, replaced by discontent and malice. "You want to live forever? Fine then, your wish shall be granted."

Rushing forward, the Dark Lord grasped the human's head in His soot-covered hands. He squeezed, the human writhing in His grip—trapped, fully comprehending that, if the Dark Lord wished to, He could crush his skull. "Immortality is yours, human! You shall live until the end of time. Death will never come for you; Azrael will never learn of your soul. Montague Saint-Orlant… you are cursed to age without the relief of eternal peace. The gates of Heaven nor the pits of Hell will ever open for your call. You will rot as you live, as your bones turn to dust—you will live until life itself ends without a body. This is your immortality, Montague."

As hands left him, Montague crumpled to his knees—gasping ragged breaths as the curse wrapped itself around every morsel of his body. He looked down at his shaking hands, cursing. "What have you done to me? I remain old. *Weak*. You were to save me—bestow unto me eternity. I can't spend eternity like this!"

He Who Bleeds

"You must know by now to be incredibly specific with demons. We like to find loopholes—if you were smarter, you would have asked for eternal *youth*. Though I'm finding you mortals are oft so preoccupied with your own self you ignore the wider picture." The fallen angel laughed, short and sweet—far more preoccupied with the sharpness of His nails. "Thou asked for immortality, so it is thine—youth was not a clause discussed."

"Bastard! You—you did this on purpose." Montague forced himself to his feet. Digging into his pocket, he retrieved a rosary, presenting the iron cross before himself. "Deus, cui próprium est miseréri sem—"

Fingers burrowed their way into Montague's waste-spewing mouth, severing his tongue from the root with sharp claws. The Dark Lord held the saliva-slick tongue between two fingers, studying it before taking a large bite from the muscle. He chewed, savoring—ignoring the gargled screams coming from Montague. The second half of the tongue was offered to Aurélien.

The muscle was still warm in his hand, soaked in blood, and as he bit into it, Aurélien found it was not unlike a heifer's. He consumed it with gluttony, satisfied as the meat hit his stomach. Aurélien looked at the sniveling, pathetic old man at their feet and felt nothing but discontent and hatred. Here was the creature, as he was not nearly human enough to call such anymore, who stole his life—who kept him captive like a plaything, who enjoyed his split confusion. Part of Aurélien longed to crush his skull in, to see what the muck inside tasted like when he dipped his fingers inside.

"Little Love, are you quite alright?" Celio asked, clinging to his arm as if to guide him away from the all-consuming thoughts.

"Quite so. Tonight has—well, I needn't say it. I simply wish to rest and get my fill of incubus. Might you know where I can source one?" Aurélien placed his hand on the small of Celio's back, feeling him shiver in excitement.

"I know a very willing incubus," the lilithspawn purred.

Montague, in all of his screaming and agonized bleating, clung to the Dark Lord's chiton. The Dark Lord scowled, shoving the man off of him "Begone, creature, do not sully my sight. You have gotten what you wanted; must you be so greedy?"

Blood ran down Montague's chin, speckling onto the Dark Lord's chiton as he tried to speak. His lip curled up and He pushed the man down, stomping onto his skull with one hard kick. The skin broke, filling the room with the delicious scent of blood. It was not enough and Aurélien spent several moments watching the Morning Star crush the once mortal man into a pool of minced meat for daring to touch Him. Aurélien was not deterred by the sight, holding no kind memories or thoughts for the man he called father for three decades, but jealousy over being the one to crush him so beautifully.

The Dark Lord tilted His head back, wiping away the blood from His cheek. The motion only served to smear the fluid around more, but He didn't seem to notice. "Let us go home, my son. I am positively starving!"

†Conviction†

Countless nights had been spent since childhood pondering the concept of Hell. At that time, Aurélien could have never guessed that he was the son of the Morning Star. No sane child pondered if he was a devilspawn. Arriving in Hell was not fire and brimstone, but cold shadows that enveloped the three demons. Hell itself had nary a pit to be seen, instead a strange copy of the world above presented itself to him, a mix of centuries and regions of architecture unsullied by the endless rains. In the distance he spied a recreation of the Hanging Gardens of Babylon, strange structures and temples dotted the streets, so many in truth that Aurélien's mind could hardly keep up. It would not take him entirely by surprise to find that the Garden of Eden had fallen into Hell along with Eve's sins.

Aurélien looked around in a daze, draped only in a robe the Dark Lord had presented him before their descent. Even the strange color of the sky above was a challenge to process, darker than pitch, hazed by distant smoke and tinted by the color of fire.

They arrived before a temple-like building, made of strange materials, and accented with what Aurélien could only call black marble—or perhaps it was onyx. The Dark Lord paid no mind to the pause in His son's steps, walking up the front stairs with long strides.

"Welcome home, Aurélien. It is hardly much, but on such short notice, it is all I had available. Rest here for as long as you wish. When you are ready, come to the palace—we have much to discuss." The Dark Lord smiled, and, before Aurélien could say his piece, vanished from sight.

As He disappeared from view, Aurélien's shoulders dropped. Aches running bone deep burrowed even furrow, pulsing throughout his body. The wounds may have been healed, but the sting of agony lingered.

"You need rest," Celio reiterated, placing a hand on Aurélien's arm, guiding him through his new residence. The estate was sprawling, each room elegant and finely furnished with handmade tiles laid out in mosaics. Upon the walls were tapestries depicting scenes from the Bible. Aurélien recognized each: the fall, the serpent, the gardens.

Events the Dark Lord had a hand in.

Events that his father planned in one way or another.

Aurélien had given the Bible thought many times in his life. When one's life revolves around the priest leading the sermons, it was difficult not to think about the text itself. The strangeness of his own actuality was not lost on the devilspawn. Irony, one may call it. To lust for a servant of the false Lord whilst being the son of the true Lord. He would laugh if it was anyone else's tale.

After decades, Aurélien finally had his answers. His truth. He finally felt whole.

Celio stopped before a closed door, cupping Aurélien's cheek. It was only then that Aurélien came back to himself. "Little Love?"

"Hm?" Aurélien placed his hand over Celio's, kissing the inside of his wrist.

"Are you faring well? You were quiet. I worry when you are."

The devilspawn nodded his head. The last days were catching up to him, he felt as bogged down as a ship run aground. "I could do with some rest. Join me, won't you?"

"If you asked me to carve out my heart and feed it to you, I would not dare to hesitate. Sleeping beside you in a temple devoted to the Dark Prince will not be a bother." Celio looked at him with such an earnest expression, fully prepared to draw a dagger to remove the beating heart from his infernal chest.

Aurélien adored this little incubus of his and couldn't help but smile despite how tired he was. If he had the energy, he'd take him against the door to their bedrooms. "Your meat is sweet, worth every bite, but not as sweet as the sounds you make when you fuck yourself on my cock."

Celio shivered in excitement. It had been days since he last fed this precious pet of his, he would be as hungry as Aurélien was, if not more. He opened the door beside them and all but dragged Aurélien inside. "You tease me like your life depends on it, Little Love. We're too tired, we'd be rutting fruitlessly. You deserve to have a proper welcome to Hell."

As they passed through the doorway, dozens of candles lit themselves, burning bright with pure Hellfire. The bedrooms opened onto a large terrace and, despite how tired Aurélien was, he meandered out to gaze upon Hell. The large, canopied bed was ignored in favor of gazing at the lights flickering in windows far below. Aurélien wondered if these descending hills and slopes with homes built into the sides were the layers of Hell that Dante spoke of.

"Beautiful, isn't it?" Celio asked, looking out at the millions of souls living their own unique lives below. Aurélien occasionally had the thought when he sat atop towering buildings in the heart of London. Each person he saw had their own story to tell and very few would ever spare him a glance—this was made even more apparent when one is perched like a bird high above. Rarely did a human look skywards. Yet here, in Hell, was it any different?

"It is. I think the air is cleaner than back in London." Celio only laughed so Aurélien continued. "This is your home, isn't it? Must be nice to be back."

"Strange is one way to describe it. I'm still a fairly young demon, so being away for years didn't feel as quick as it would to an older incubus. It's nice to see my house didn't get stolen and the Dark Lord even had it maintained. He really can be so kind."

"Oh? This is your temple?"

Celio leaned back against the terrace railing. "Mhm. A gift from the Dark Lord. I thought when I fell out of favor He would take it back, but my worldly possessions are exactly where I left them."

In the distance he could see a pair of winged demons flying by. "How old are you, anyways? You know quite literally everything about me, but I know little about you."

The lilithspawn thought for a while, counting on his fingers. "Seventy-three."

Aurélien made a small acknowledging sound. "You really are young."

"So sayeth the demon who has yet to be a human's middling age."

He Who Bleeds

Aurélien smiled and drew Celio in for a kiss. "Let's go to bed, pet."

✝✝✝

If there was a morning in Hell, it came all too quickly for Aurélien's liking. The bed they occupied was warm and fairly comfortable, swathed in furs and silks. Celio laid sprawled against Aurélien, his face pressed against his chest. It had been hours since he had woken but couldn't find the energy to move his incubus out of the way.

Aurélien's fingers wove into Celio's long hair, watching it slip from his grip before he'd pick a strand up to twist around again. The silence of the estate gave Aurélien a good deal of time to think about his future. Mostly, if there was a point in considering a future when he would continue to exist until the world crumbled in on itself. Time, as a whole, had very little meaning anymore.

When he still held onto the blissful ignorance that walked hand in hand with humanity, Aurélien had been in awe of the knowledge that he would live to see the turn of the century. 1900 was a far-off year full of technology and art he couldn't dream of—now, however, seeing the year 4000 was well within the realm of possibilities.

Celio, as well, was thought upon. The concept of love foreign to him, such as it would be until the end of days, yet there was the overwhelming desire to keep his little false priest. Keep him safe, *his*—it was a brewing jealousy he couldn't push away.

"Are you up?" Celio asked, his voice quiet and drenched in sleep. The tone brushed aside any jealous ideations Aurélien had, replacing it with the throb of his cock. A hand traced the planes of Aurélien's chest, past the trail of dark hair and to the waistband of his linen trousers. "Oh, both of you are up I see."

"You cast blame on me? I woke with the most dashing lilithspawn in my arms. It was tortuous to feel you against me without being able to lay my claim on your flesh." Aurélien's hips rolled into the warm, welcomed touch. Celio's lips were just out of reach of his own, his eyes blown wide with his own desire. When Celio fed, his eyes glowed the most beautiful gold—reminding Aurélien of well-polished metal, which complimented his incubus' skin in ways he could never put into words. Aurélien was aware he was no poet nor was he an artist or craftsman who could capture the muse before him with great accuracy. Though, with aeons before them, perhaps he could learn.

"No blame, Little Love, simply enjoyment. I had the most delicious dream regarding you… myself… and the Dark Lord." Celio stroked Aurélien's cock to fullness, his slim fingers tracing over the length in a teasing, devious manner.

"I'd much prefer not to speak of the Dark Lord while you fuck yourself on my cock."

"You had no problem tasting His tongue yesterday," Celio reminded, much to Aurélien's chagrin.

"He is quite hypnotic. I lost myself in Him."

Celio laughed and began to mouth along Aurélien's neck. "He has that effect on us lesser demons. What He wants, He gets. I only tease, Little Love. Though, I must say, watching the two of you was exhilarating. No display has ever been so erotic."

"Celio… you may have me today. I am yours. As a reward for quite literally everything you have done." Aurélien removed his hands from Celio's body, draping them above his head in surrender. "I want you to devour me. Feast until you are full and satiated."

The lilithspawn snapped back, staring wide-eyed at Aurélien. "You don't mean that."

"Well, there is one condition."

"Tell me," Celio demanded breathlessly. He looked as precious as a kitten who was presented with a bowl of milk. Celio was curtained by his long hair that hid his beautiful, tanned skin from Aurélien's eyes.

"As long as I can feel you around my cock, you can have your feast."

Celio slipped off the bed and began rummaging through a chest he produced from the side of the bed. From within he pulled a band of thick ribbon, purple in color. He quickly returned to sit between Aurélien's thighs and, with the use of the purple ribbon, secured his hands to the headboard. Aurélien allowed himself to be guided, a playful smile upon his face.

"I can tear out of this in an instant, Celio." Aurélien couldn't help but remind his little incubus.

"Do your utmost not to tear free. It's so much less fun when you do." Celio ran his hands over Aurélien's pectorals, thumbing over his nipples with slow strokes. He watched them perk with rapt fascination.

"Anything you desire, Father Beausoliel."

Celio giggled, laying a kiss on his sternum. "I desire many things, Little Love, and you are written at the top of that list."

"Pray tell, what is line two and three?"

"Your cock." The kisses trailed lower. Celio's tail wrapped around his thigh, stroking slowly to tease him. His cock was already erect, throbbing with neglect. "And your hole."

Aurélien laid back against the pillows, closing his eyes to enjoy the euphoria his starving lilithspawn was about to wring out of him.

"You are truly crafted from the purest of stone." Celio's oil-slicked hand wrapped around his cock, stroking slowly. The drag was bliss, drawing a sigh from Aurélien.

"And you from brimstone."

Pleasure was one of Celio's gifts, his entire purpose on earth was to feast on the pleasure of man. Aurélien was all too willing to feed the addiction his incubus possessed. He himself craved his false priest like a fish craved water. Eternity seemed less daunting with someone so positively distracting by his side.

As Celio's kisses came to his cock, his mouth replaced his hand. Sweet bliss washed over Aurélien as a wet, hot mouth enveloped him.

"Celio—" His thoughts were halted by the feeling of the lilithspawn swallowing him down to the root, burying his nose in dark hair and musk. Daring fingers circled at his hole, slick and welcomed. A short, unmuffled moan slipped from the devilspawn.

When his mouth left Aurélien's cock, Celio mouthed sloppily along the shaft. "Good boy. Don't hold back. Let me hear you."

Two fingers thrust inside, and another moan was forced out. Celio's devious smile only grew. "You like that, huh? Having your ass played with?"

"Must we speak?"

Celio laughed, nipping at the meat of his inner thigh. His fangs pricked his skin, blood beading up quickly, which was greedily licked away. "You don't have to answer. It was purely rhetorical. I can feel how you clench around my fingers—how your hole sucks me in."

Instead of continuing his lustful line of questioning, Celio licked Aurélien from base to tip before swallowing his erection. His skilled fingers neither ceased nor paused their thrusting, sending tingles throughout Aurélien's body. He tugged at his bindings but did not tear the ribbon. The incubus spit coating his cock was like venom, rushing through his veins and turning him into a brainless lump only good for feasting from. "Fuck—Celio, you better be satiated after this."

The scorching hot mouth popped off of his cock. Celio looked up at him, his mouth slick with his own spit. "I will be full for days."

Another finger was added and then another, until Aurélien was gasping and pathetically thrusting his hips into the loose grip of Celio's hand. His body was slick with precum, incubus spit, and oil—the heat in the room was unbearable, as electric as a storm. He needed more, but Celio kept his orgasm at bay with all the practiced grace of a trained Parisian whore.

"More," Aurélien demanded, grinding his hips down to experience just a touch more pleasure.

"Yes, my Dark Prince, anything you desire shall be yours. More you shall have." Celio pulled his fingers out, eyes trained on the motion. A pink tongue darted out, licking his lips as if to taste the view. Oil was applied generously to his hand before Celio pressed his fist into Aurélien's gaped hole, which pulsed in its own greedy desire.

Aurélien's head fell back onto the pillows, inhaling so deeply his lungs burned. The stretch was delicious, and he was incapable of quieting the moans he released. Celio watched him like a Shakespearean play, his eyes flickering from his hand to Aurélien's face.

Celio brought his free hand to stroke Aurélien's erection, his other pumping slow into that stretched space. "I knew you would look beautiful with your legs spread wide, Little Love."

"N-Not as beautiful as you." Aurélien choked out his words before a choked moan tore from his throat in the shape of Celio's name. Cum striped across Celio's hand, drops landing on Aurélien's lower stomach. "C-Celio!"

The lilithspawn stroked him through his orgasm, milking pearls from his unflagging erection. "That's it, cum for me."

Celio gently removed his hand, bending low to lick away the seed from Aurélien's body.

Aurélien struggled to catch his breath, but slowly came down from his orgasm. His false priest had kissed away the mess, Celio's eyes glowing bright.

Licking his lips, Celio purred his desires. "More. More, Little Love, I still hunger."

"Take from me, have of me. Feast from my body." Aurélien used his foot to nudge Celio up. "Fuck yourself on my cock until you're a mess."

"You sound just like the Dark Lord." Celio kissed him deeply, pressing his tongue against his. He straddled the devilspawn, letting Aurélien thrust against his plentiful rear.

Aurélien longed to place his hands upon Celio's unholy form, spread his plump peaks and fuck into the space between them. He tugged gently on the ribbon binding his hands above his head, considering if he should tear himself free. That was, until his thoughts were derailed by the press of something thin between his ass. Celio's tail teased around his hole for a moment before thrusting inside.

"Devilish bastard," Aurélien scolded with no real malice behind it. He relished in the feeling of Celio's tail fucking into him and he only wished to return the favor. "Fuck yourself on my cock already."

Celio hardly hesitated, adjusting himself so he could take Aurélien within himself in one smooth motion. His own cock bobbed between his legs, throbbing from neglect. "A–hah—A-Au—Ah, Little Love. You are so deep inside me!"

The incubus raised himself before coming down hard, again and again until he was a breathless, blubbering mess. All the while, his tail fucked itself in and out of Aurélien's gaped hole. Aurélien's mind was washed of anything aside from the moans and whimpers of his false priest. Watching his expressions change with each slide of his cock was enough to fuel Aurélien's fantasies for generations.

"F-Fuck me, please—take me!" Celio begged, eyes filled with tears on the verse of spilling over.

Ribbon was an exceptionally easy material to tear through and Aurélien wasted no time in tearing his hands free from their bindings. Celio's hips were in his hands within a moment, slipping down to spread his ass apart.

"Mh—bastard, t-that was my fa-vorite ribbon!" Celio's laughter was cut short by a hard thrust, tumbling moans overtaking any words he wished to say. He pressed his face into the crook of Aurélien's neck and accepted everything given to him.

Aurélien fucked up into the welcoming, tight heat with little regard for Celio's pleasure. As his second orgasm edged closer, his movements became less fluid, more erratic as he chased the impeding high.

Celio cried out his name, arching his back as he came between them during one particular hard thrust. His seed smeared across their bodies, sticky and hot.

"Au—! O' praise, praise!"

Aurélien thrust deep into his heat and came, biting into Celio's shoulder to muffle his cry of pleasure.

They remained tangled together until the aphrodisiac known as incubus spittle dissipated. Celio used the strips of ribbon to wipe away the cum on their stomachs.

"Is this how all princes of Hell are welcomed?" Aurélien asked, rolling over to watch Celio as he settled into a comfortable cocoon of furs and silk.

"Only the ones I'm fond of."

Aurélien smiled to himself, kissing Celio's forehead. "Satisfied?"

"Beyond satisfied, Little Love. I want for naught."

†The Dark Prince†

Demonic customs were as foreign to Aurélien as life beneath the crashing waves of the sea. Thus, he followed the instructions given by those who poised themselves in authoritative positions—those with wounds upon their backs, which they showed off with low cut chitons and other various wrappings that would leave human gentry blushing. He learned their names but dared not repeat them in full: Beelzebub. Mammon. Belial. Asmodeus. Each more beautiful than the last, clinging to their angelic beauty in a way no sin-born demon did. He forced out the syllables of their names until his Heaven-fallen family laughed.

One demon, however, was unwelcomed in his consistent pestering. Axædus sat within the chamber with him as servants bustled about with cloth, needles, and thread—measuring every angle of his body to create the perfect ceremonial garb. His long hair had been tightly pleated away from his face, fixed with bells that rang with each movement of his head. He wore human-made clothing, a century old in style—French, as far as Aurélien was able to discern, deep royal blue in color embroidered with black and silver thread. "I must say, you've done well for yourself, brother."

"Well. That is certainly one way to describe it."

"Not all of us had Father running to our rescue," Axædus remarked. "Some of us had to wait until our clients were satisfied. Mine lived another sixty years after the contract was signed."

Aurélien glanced back at his brother in the mirror, noting the forlorn expression. "What was your contract?"

"Born to a whore who wished to become the mistress of the whore house. Father wasn't as picky back then with his mates. I was no better than an incubus. I was five when I had my first client." A palpable silence filled the room. "I prayed to every damned god there was to make it stop, but not one would answer me. Nobody wanted to help the son of the Dark Lord. Unlike you, I had no help, no pretty lilithspawn to distract me from the pain."

Aurélien rolled his eyes. This brother of his was unbelievable, truly spouting nonsense that didn't pertain to Aurélien in the slightest. "I never asked Father for help. I never asked *you* for help. Don't put your blame on me for something centuries ago."

"I don't. I only blame myself for not being strong enough." The second general sighed and held out his hand until a servant placed a cigarette between his fingers. He brought it to his lips and took a long drag. "You are simply exceptionally... lucky."

"I don't believe demons have a single ounce of luck, Ax."

A laugh. Axædus' eyes darted down to his lap where he placed all of his focus on the end of his braid. "Another thing dear grandfather has taken from us."

Aurélien made a questioning noise until his brother elaborated.

"Have you never thought about it? You truly are beef-witted. God is real, brother, and he has forsaken us all. We are birthed from his favorite angel, who is he but our grandfather? God never helped me. He never helped you."

"God is dead as far as I'm concerned."

He Who Bleeds

✝✝✝

Days had begun to be lost on Aurélien soon after his arrival in Hell. As far as he knew, only a few short weeks had passed, yet the possibility of years was not out of the question. Until this day, he remained within his bed with Celio, and if not there, wandering the streets and alleyways of Hell with his lilithspawn trailing close behind.

This day, however, was unlike any other. Aurélien had been dressed by servant upon servant, each more uniquely demonic than the last. He wore deep red cloth spun from the silk of a spider demon, which one servant informed could not be cut nor burned with ordinary weapons or fire. It felt soft against his flesh, thin and cool to the touch. A chainmail was added next, and if Aurélien was truthful, he had not listened to the explanation on its creation—only nodding his head as it was fastened onto him. It hung from his body like water, lightweight despite its length, hitting the calves of his armored boots.

A myriad of armor pieces were placed onto his person, pitch black in color and spiked at his shoulders—scaled pieces fell around his hips like a skirt to protect his tail. Decorative pieces of the crimson spider demon silk were added to his hips and at his back in the form of a cape. When he looked into the mirror, ceremonial sword in hand, he saw a man he scarcely recognized. Aurélien found he appeared stronger and fiercer than he ever had before.

"You are stunning, my Dark Prince," Celio praised, pressing a kiss to his cheek. "The Dark Lord is expecting you; we need to hurry."

208

Dorian Valentine

Within the center of Hell sat the Morning Star, looking out over the hordes of demons who came to view the newest son—to deem him worthy of his demonic lineage. The coronation of a new demonic prince was a rare occurrence, one that occurred only once every millennium, if the stars aligned and the Dark Lord had enough luck.

A hoarde lay before Aurélien, rows upon rows of demons staring back at him as an orchestra blared music loud enough to challenge the trumpets of angels. They parted like the red sea before him, bowing low with their bodies but not with their heads, all looking up at him expectantly whilst he walked by. Some brave reached outwards to touch his armor and Aurélien sliced away the offending hands with his blade.

There was no outrage for such an action, only the frenzied, cannibalistic feasting on those marked unworthy by the Dark Lord's newest son. Aurélien salivated at the scent of blood in the air. He wanted to turn on his heel and join the feast—to sink his fangs into the warm flesh and tear until his stomach bulged from his gluttony. He forced himself to continue walking forwards towards the Dark Lord's throne.

Aeons seemed to pass before he was able to walk up the steps towards his father. The Dark Lord sat upon a throne crafted of bone, iron, and the rotting wings of angels. Surrounding him were his brothers, some he had yet to meet along with the Heaven-fallen demons who claimed the title of prince as well. Before their awesome might, Aurélien knelt, his armor clanked against the marble floor. He knelt within a circle scrawled onto the marble with blood, as instructed previously.

As the Dark Lord stood, there was the chorus of shifting bodies—all those in attendance rising in order to bow towards their true Lord. Lucifer raised a hand, and a second wave of sounds came, the grinding of armor, the clinking of bijoux.

"One thousand mortal years have passed since we welcomed a new general into our ranks. Our Prince Enyo has been in Hell for a millennium now. It feels like just yesterday that we welcomed her. Time passes so very quickly for mortals." The Dark Lord cast a glance at a woman sitting behind him. Prince Enyo was tall and muscular with sharp features to match, her moonlight pale skin seemed to glow in the light of the Hellfire lanterns. She nodded her head towards their father, her golden hair done up in braids that reminded Aurélien of iron age artworks.

"Today is an auspicious day. Aurélien will be reborn from the ashes of his humanity." A small satchel appeared within His hand, which was opened with care. The ashes within were sprinkled around him by two lesser demons.

The Dark Lord smiled solemnly and with the sharp claw of His finger, slit His wrist. The blood of the fallen angel was collected into a crystal chalice. The bleeding ceased the moment He deemed there to be enough blood in the cup. The ashes were lit by a servant, a burning ring of fire around him. The heat warmed his skin pleasantly.

"Drink of my blood, be remade from within. Burn away the last of your humanity." The Dark Lord offered the chalice to Aurélien. He opened his mouth and allowed the blood to be poured onto his tongue. Aurélien dare not waste a single drop.

Rebirth.

Rebirth was agony. Pain tore through his body like lightning bolts, scorching away the very fibers of his being. Aurélien kept his mouth sealed, not even huffing his discontent. If the Dark Lord continued to speak while his body transfigured itself, Aurélien was unable to tell. He heard nothing over the buzz in his ears and the screeching of singers within the orchestra.

Aurélien healed and repaired for moments—perhaps hours. He knew naught when his eyes refocused and his ears ceased hearing tea kettle whistles.

"He who bleeds for the crown shall be blessed with my strength—my power—my wisdom." A crown of iron thorns was placed onto Aurélien, pricking the skin until drops of blood formed beneath its weight. They ran in ruby rivulets down his face, which he turned upwards to gaze at the Dark Lord, his infernal father. "I present unto you all, my loyal subjects, the Dark Prince Aurélien, ruler of thirteen legions in Hell, general in my Infernal Army. May he go forth in sin."

About the Author

Dorian Valentine is a LGBT+ author living in a haunted house in rural Connecticut. He loves to write about vampires, fae and gothic themes—and he can't be damned to write anything else. When he isn't writing you can find him bothering his two cats, walking in the cemetery, and scaring the locals.

More by Valentine:

THE EASTERN QUARTER'S MANA

Vol. I: Rosemary & Iron
Vol. II: These Bittersweet Vines

New England is a rather strange place for religion, soaked in everything from Catholicism to Witchcraft. You can be drawn in by the beauty of Notre Dame while also finding the Satanic Temple along the way. I think the Puritans would hate that very much (this book too, as well).

He Who Bleeds is for anyone who has ever felt smothered by the church, by society—by life. Please know that you are much stronger than you think. I hope one day that you can find a way to do more than just survive in this world.

There are many people I'd like to thank, so I'll keep it short. Thank you to my alpha & beta readers, Sky, Achilles, Finn, Taylor, Harvey & Shane. Without you this would be a total mess still. Also a huge thank you to Elle Porter for helping me get the ebook up and running! And, of course, to my friends who still listened to me talk about my little creatures even though this is my third novel and by now it has to be boring.

Thank you to anyone who picked up this novel. Your support means more than you could ever imagine. May you feel free to live as yourself, though perhaps not as free as our dear protagonist. Please don't eat people, some consider it to be very rude.

Your disastrous author,
      Dorian Valentine